Addicted to Him 4
By Linette King

Addicted To Him 4
-Written By-
Linette King

Copyright © 2016 by True Glory Publications
Published by True Glory Publications
Join our Mailing List by texting TrueGlory to
64600 or click here
http://optin.mobiniti.com/V2Yr

Facebook: **Author Linette King**

*This novel is a work of fiction. Any resemblances to
actual events, real people, living or dead,
organizations, establishments or locales are
products of the author's imagination. Other names,
characters, places, and incidents are used
fictitiously.*

Cover Design: Michael Horne
Editor: Tamyra L. Griffin

the views of the publisher and the publisher hereby disclaims any responsibility for them.

Acknowledgements

First of all, I have to give thanks to God who is the head of my household for without you I am nothing. To God be the glory!

To my children: Aaliyah, Alannah and Jaye, I love you guys so freaking much! I'll go to war against anyone about you guys! If you don't remember anything else, keep God first and everything will fall into place.

To my family: Mama, you are by far the craziest lady I've ever met and it's getting worse, but I wouldn't trade you for nothing in the world. Pooh, you always look out for me. When people come against me, you get mad as if they said those things to you. LOL I'll always have your back because you always have mine. Oliver, I can't name a soul that I'm closer to than you. You're my big brother, always have been, always will be. I love you guys!

To my friends: Jasmine, half of the time I don't know what to say about you. LOL You are so freaking silly it's unreal. Never change. Trinisha, girl them conversations we be having always have you saying, "Um, I don't wanna know that!" LOL But what are friends for? Precious, big dog, you all the way 100 and you never switch up and I just love that about your extra crazy self. We can go for a while without talking and jump back like it was nothing. We both know that tends to happen when everybody's grown and have other things to do. I love you guys!

Shoutouts: Big Bruh! Brandon B2Smoove Miles, I wish you nothing but greatness with your clothing line. I know you got this and you know sis will help in any way she can! #BlueHunnidGang

Danielle Sanders! I know you're going to be awesome with this new hairline! You are a very intelligent, strong, business minded young woman! #KaiBella will be everything you've ever dreamed of and more.

Teago Brown! My mfn G! Y'all make sure you look out for AGO Productionz! Big homie has a lot going on, literally! This man is a jack of all trades! I see his vision and I know he's going to take off like a rocket! The man is brilliant! Lookout world! Contact him @agoproductionz@gmail.com for anything regarding promotions, planning and event hosting!

To my readers: This is book number 8 and y'all are still rocking with me! Shameek saw something in me that I didn't see in myself and you guys seem to love it! Make sure you guys find me on Facebook because I'm always available for any questions you may have. Thanks for reading! I love you!

Everything in this book is a work of fiction. I never talk about an actual event or person. If it appears that way, it's purely coincidental. Enjoy!

Table Of Contents

Michelle gave her mission of killing Tamia a break with hopes of the police eventually leaving her alone; so she will be free to kill Tamia and claim Rashard as her man. She has faith that once Lisa finds out that Dre is dead, she won't snitch on her for killing Bo. She has no idea that Lisa is dead or that Bo is hanging on by a thread of faith.

Armani just found out she was pregnant the morning she decided to turn over a new leaf and help Tamia and Candy reconnect. She had hopes that she and Dave would raise their child together but now she doesn't know if she's going to keep it, considering he's still with his wife.

Tamia tried her hardest to keep Chardae alive until the ambulance showed up, while Rashard stood in the same spot in a state of shock. She succeeded. Unfortunately, the baby didn't make it. Now Rashard and Tamia have to figure out what they're going to do about their relationship.

*　　*　　*　　*　　*

"Sir are you ready to tell us who you are?" The nurse asked and the patient shook his head. "Well we are about to discharge you, do you have anyone that can come get you?" she asked and he shook his head. "Okay, well tomorrow you will be cleared to go." she said then walked out of the room.

The nurse walked down to the nurse's station to talk to Dr. James about the patient they call "The Miracle Patient." He was shot in the back and had a collapsed lung from the gunshot wound. When the paramedics arrived, he had no heartbeat but they were able to resuscitate him. He was on a ventilator for almost two weeks before he could breathe on his own again. When they first pulled the tube from his mouth, he tried to talk but his throat was so dry. The nurse gave him a cup of water, pen and paper; and he wrote a message.
"Tamia, I'm coming."
Was all it said, but the nurse had no idea who Tamia was and nobody came to visit him his entire time there.

"He still won't tell us his name." the nurse said to the doctor in charge of his care. The doctor simply nodded his head and walked off, completely unaware of the danger he would be putting someone in by not getting authorities involved.

<u>Armani</u> .

One year later….

The struggle has been real! Man I have to salute every single mom out there, because this shit is not easy! As I stared into the eyes of my son, Armad, I couldn't help but to admire him. He's two months old and is the only bright spot in my life. Well somewhat of a bright spot.

Somewhere in this past year, Tamia and I were able to patch up our friendship with a few lies and half assed apologies, but it's cool. She agreed to help me with Armad, but then moved her little happy go lucky ass to Atlanta! So that's where we are now.

The crazy thing is, I have no idea where the bitch lives! She claims to have forgiven me and she's Armad's God mother, but I've never been to her house. I've never even had an invitation extended. It's cool though, because I'll get there soon.

I smiled down at Armad as he giggled and made slurpy noises. He tried hard as hell to grab the large earrings that I was wearing but he couldn't reach them. "Hey mommy's juicy man!" I cooed in his face. He always thought it was the funniest thing ever when I would say that to him.

My phone began to ring from the kitchen counter, so I got up and made my way over to it. I sighed heavily and rolled my eyes once I saw that it was Dave. He had been trying to get me to come see him, or to allow him to come see me since we moved here six months ago; but I wasn't budging. I'm a new person these days. The Armani that was sleeping with other people's men for money, is dead and gone. I just hope I'm done reaping the karma from all of the seeds I've sowed. I shook my head as I answered the phone.

"Hello?" I answered the phone clearly annoyed. I had an annoyed expression on my face and I'm pretty sure he could tell I was annoyed when I first answered the phone.

Armad began to wiggle in my arms as he tried to grab the phone out of my hand. He's the most active two-month old baby I'd ever encountered! Wait, I think he's the only baby I've encountered period! Funny!

"I miss you." Dave said in a raspy voice.

I knew right off that he didn't miss me as a person. He misses what I use to make that meat do! He misses how I used to suck it with no hands. He misses how I use to make my pussy squirt on it then lick my juices back off.

"Yea. I don't doubt it." I said with a smirk on my face.

I began to bounce Armad slightly as I cradled him with one arm. I could tell he was getting a bit cranky. I'm sure he will be fussing for a bottle shortly.

"What's that supposed to mean?" Dave asked with too much bass in his voice for my liking.

"Nigga it means calm yo rabbit ass down before I put you on my block list!" I snapped. I must have been too loud because Armad started screaming at the top of his lungs. "Ugh!" I said, because I was completely frustrated at this point.

I hung the phone up and bounced Armad just a little harder as I hummed the tune of Twinkle, Twinkle Little Star. It normally works, but it wasn't working for me. For the life of me I couldn't get him to calm down. The doorbell rang and I sighed heavily as I made my way to the door with my hollering son.

I'd never been happier to see Tamia in my life! She had a worried expression on her face as she took Armad out of my arms.

"If I was a butterfly, butterfly, butterfly. If I was a butterfly, I would fly real high." she sang in his face.

His cries started to settle as she continued to sing a song I had never heard, but knew I needed to learn. After his cries stopped, he smiled up at her as she made her way all the way into my home.

"Where'd you learn that song?" I asked her. "Back on the coast. There was this lady, Pooh I think they called her. She would sing that song to babies and they would hush and smile." she explained. I nodded my head because now I need to learn that song.

She cradled Armad close to her chest as she carried him to his room. I followed her because I didn't know what she was doing. Rashard bought this house for me, but that didn't give Tamia the right to walk through it like she owns the place.

She laid him on the changing table in his room and changed his diaper. He cooed and smiled as he looked up at her. *"He never looks at me that way. How can she come in and take my only bright spot?"*

Tamia

I could feel Armani staring a hole in the side of my face, but I dared not mention it. See it's times like this that she does this shit that makes me keep my distance. Yes, I help her with Armad, but that's because he's innocent in all of this. He didn't ask to have her as a mother, so I help whenever I can. Not to mention, Armad is an awesome distraction from my personal life. Rashard and I have been kind of rocky since that whole Chardae incident last year in the kitchen of my beautiful home. I think I was more pissed off than I was hurt though.

He told me that she got pregnant before he and I established anything and I would have believed him, had he told me about it. I guess that was too much like right for a nigga like Rashard! So I'm guessing that's why he bought me a house. He wanted to soften the blow of someone else having his child.

I shook my head to rid myself of those thoughts as I changed Armad's clothes.

"How are you?" I asked Armani.

She hasn't had any dick since we moved out here and it shows all up and through her attitude! She was already hard to deal with when she's her normal self. Now imagine how hard it is to deal with built up Armani. Armani that hasn't had any dick in six months.

"I'm good." she said then turned on the heels of her feet and walked away. She's so over the top with everything these days.

I packed Armad a small bag so we could spend some time together. I strapped him down in his car seat, draped the bag over my shoulder and carried him into the living room.

"Where yall going now?" Armani asked with an attitude. I looked down at Armad because he was fast asleep.

"I'm going to give you a break. Maybe we will go to the park or something. Get out and have a little fun." I said to her.

I stood there patiently as I waited for her smart comment but she just smiled.

"When are you going to bring him back?" she asked. I looked down at him and thought for a few seconds. "We will be back tomorrow." I said and her jaw hit the floor.

I knew she couldn't believe that I was going to keep him overnight, but I needed company. Rashard hardly ever comes homes these days. I think he's doing what he was doing back in Detroit. He told me all about how he made his money so either he was doing that, or he was fucking off somewhere.

It's crazy though because every time I fuss about his unavailability, he hits me with, "You shouldn't want a man that's always got time. A nigga with a lot of time ain't got no money baby." I could hear his stupid ass saying that right now!

Armani walked us to my new candy paint, all black BMW 5 series. I loved everything about the car from the customized floor mats, to the leather seats with seat warmers that I didn't need at the moment.

"Girl this car still smells new." Armani said as she leaned in to give Armad a kiss on his mouth. I frowned my face up in disgust as I bit my tongue. "Hmm mhh." I said to keep from telling her how to parent her own child.

Rashard bought me this car back in March, the day before Armani had Armad. The only reason I haven't left Rashard yet is because I love him and he's taking care of Armani, Armad and myself. Neither of us have to pay a thing and that's how I need it to stay for now.

Okay I lied, the things he does for me isn't the only reason why I haven't left him. It's also the things he does to me! That man will have me pissed off to the max, come home, stick his tongue in my ass, fuck the shit out of me and I end up on a cloud. Every single time I get mad at him, the sex is off the chain! That's why I get mad over everything! If a light bulb goes out I be in his face like, "Really nigga!". It's crazy but shit, that's what I have to do. It's like as long as I'm in good spirits, our sex life is good but when I'm mad…. it's fucking awesome!

"Bitch you don't hear me talking to you?!" Armani asked. I looked up at her because thoughts of Rashard had a bitch mind completely gone and panties completely wet.

"Naw what you say?" I asked as I stood up straight. I had subconsciously leaned over to make sure Armad was buckled in safely. I didn't miss the look she gave me and gave her an apologetic shrug of my shoulders. "Force of habit." I said as I waited for her to tell me what she was talking about.

"Dave called me again." she said as she sighed and looked off into space.

I noticed a longing look in her facial expression, but I was not about to tell her what she already knew. For one, she wanted him and two, he's unavailable. Sure he will fly her out there or fly in to see her, but he will indefinitely go back home to his wife. That's what I think about when she vents to me, but those are things she already knows.

I know you're thinking, well if she's your friend then tell her.... but you have to understand, she is not my friend. The only reason I talk to her is to make sure Armad is ok and being loved the way a child should be loved. For some reason I just don't think Armani is capable of that. She's just not a nurturing kind of person.

"And what happened?" I asked just to make conversation. I'm sure she can tell by my tone that I couldn't give a fuck about her and Dave even if I wanted to.

"I told him I would block him if he called again!" she boasted all hyped up, animated and shit. I know she claims to have changed but you know hard it is to change an old dog.

Old habits die hard and that's exactly why I keep her away from Rashard. I would hope he isn't as trifling as Amere was, but I've learned not to put anything past anyone.

"Good." I said as I walked around to the driver's side of my car.

That was my way of letting her know that I was about to go; since the fact that Armad was secured in his car seat, inside the car wasn't enough. She didn't take the hint. She followed me around to the driver's side of the car.

"Girl, I don't know what to do without my baby." she whined as she leaned her wide ass against my car. I'm used to Armani being a big, beautiful girl without trying but Armad has taken her body down through there! I needed my girl to join a gym immediately and get back to being the Armani she was before she started sleeping with Amere. That's the only Armani I want to deal with.

"Join a book club or a gym or something." I suggested with no pun intended. Okay, hell yea I meant it but that was my subtle way of saying, *"Bitch you been eating hella good!"* She gave me the side eye then nodded her head a little bit and stood up straight.

"Can't stand you skinny bitches!" she said and stormed back in her house. I shook my head at her and drove off for some baby and me time.

Rashard

"Oooh fuck!" she screamed out as she tried to crawl away.

"Bring that ass back over here!" I said as I grabbed her hips and snatched her back towards me. I entered her roughly and continued to knock her back out. "This pussy gushing girl damn!" I said as I slowed my pace.

Every time she came I could feel her pussy muscles squeeze my dick and she almost drained me every time.

"It's wet for you daddy!" she moaned out as she slipped her hands between her legs.

I reached over, popped her hand and she moved it out the way. I grabbed her hair and snatched her head back as I gave her long, deep, rough strokes. She tried to crawl away again, so I knew she was about to nut. Every time her nut was coming, she would try to stop it. I have no idea why she kept running from it. Her body began to tremble and she started squeezing my dick with her pussy muscles again. I felt that familiar tingle at my toes and knew I was about to nut.

Once she realized it, she started bucking back on a nigga. I felt like a bitch the way she had my body rocking. I fought hard to think about anything else because I wasn't ready to cum yet. She started squeezing me and throwing her big ass in a circle.

"Umm." I moaned out as I slapped her ass where my name is tattooed.

She moaned out and threw her ass back faster and I couldn't fight it anymore. I fucked her hard, then pulled out just before I came. I sat down on the bed as I removed the condom and caught my breath. I could feel her eyes burning through me, but I refused to acknowledge her. Once I caught my breath, I walked out to the bathroom. The only thing I had on was a condom and tube socks as I made my way down her hall.

When I made it inside of the bathroom, I poured my nut in the toilet and flushed it. I then made my way to the sink and ran water in the condom. None of the water came out so I flushed the condom and then hopped in the shower.

I walked back into the room and she was still sitting there with an attitude. She was seriously doing the fucking most! She was sitting with her back against the headboard, with her arms folded across her plump breast. I shook my head as I put my clothes back on.

"Where you going?!" she asked with an attitude.

I checked my phone to see if Tamia had called but she hadn't. I don't know what her ass been doing all day but she hadn't called me a single time!

"Home." I answered as I turned around to face her. I knew exactly what argument we were about to have, because we've had it plenty of times since I moved her here two months ago.

I bought her a high rise condo and felt so guilty about the shit that I went and bought Tamia a BMW. There was no way I would let a bitch I'm fucking outdo my girl.

"Why can't you just stay Rashard?" she asked in a whiny like voiced. I sighed heavily because I couldn't believe we were about to do this again.

"Chill man don't start." I said as I held my hand out to stop her, but it was too late. She jumped up with her titties swinging as she made her way to me aggressively.

"Don't start! Nigga did you just say don't start?! Naw nigga, don't you start! Why the fuck did you move me here huh? You want me to be your ass on the side nigga?!" she screamed in my face. I didn't respond because I was trying not to be the asshole that I use to be.

"Man. You. Better. Fucking. Answer. Me!" she said as she clapped in between each word.

"This bitch is fucking looney." I thought to myself as I continued to stare at her.

"This is not how I envisioned shit between us Rashard!" she screamed as fresh tears fell down her cheeks.

"Oh here we go." I thought to myself as I gave her a minute to get herself together.

"I didn't expect to fall in love with you." she said as she lowered her gaze to the ground. I'm sure she could see my jaw that had just hit the floor.

When I first started talking to her, she was only using me for money. Shit, I thought she'd be the perfect side chick since she had a motive! Hell I would just dish out the cash and she would dish out the ass with no feelings attached to it, but I was wrong.

"You shouldn't have." I said calmly. She looked up at me with a confused look on her face. "I got a few questions for you." I said and waited for her to acknowledge what I had just said to her.

Instead of responding, she climbed back onto her bed. "When I met you, did I have a girl?" I asked but she didn't respond. "When I asked you to move here, did I have a girl?" I asked and she still didn't respond. I could see her blood boiling as she got pissed off unrightfully so. "Is the girl that was my girl when we met still my girl now?" I asked just as calm as I was when I first spoke up. She continued to stare at me. "If you answer yes to any of those questions, why the fuck would you fall in love with me?" I asked.

My first three questions were rhetorical because there was no need in her answering questions I already knew the answer to. Now that last question, that last question was a serious fucking question. She started fucking me knowing about Tamia. She moved here knowing about Tamia. Now she's sitting her mad because I'm going home to Tamia!

I shook my head as I turned around to walk out of the door when something hit me in my back. I turned around and looked down. I saw she threw her fucking shoe at me. I looked up ready to snap out on her ass but had to dodge another shoe.

"What the fuck?!" I shouted as I ducked again.

She had thrown a lamp that shattered once it came into contact with the wall. I wanted to snap her fucking neck as I ducked out of the room and high tailed it out the door. As soon as I made it to my car, she was standing at the door wearing only a T shirt that barely covered anything up.

I crank my car up and pulled off. Now I need to go check on Tamia's ass because normally she would have called me going off by now. Hopefully, she doesn't want any dick because I just gave Natasia everything.

Yeah, I'm still fucking with the green eyed beauty. Ole gold digging turned love sick chick! I shook my head at the thought of what had just happened just as my phone started ringing. I answered it using the Bluetooth in my Bugatti. Man, I dropped $350,000 as a down payment to drive off in this beauty. Tamia said it was a foolish choice, but didn't say that shit when I pulled up in her BMW.

"Yo!" I yelled out to answer the phone.

"Ah boy! What's good fam?" Meech yelled into the phone.

Meech is my homeboy from back in the day. Back when I was the look out, he used to answer the phone calls from the old head that were in prison. When I opted to go to school so I could become a legit businessman, he decided to move off and take over Atlanta since I had Detroit on lock. Funny thing is, he's been here for years and still haven't locked down everything and now he wants my help to do just that.

"Ain't shit fam, fina go check on my lady." I said to him. He chuckled lightly but didn't say anything. "What's up?" I asked.

"Man you need to come down to DOA." he exclaimed. That may not be a bad idea.

"Iight bet." I said then disconnected the call.

Michelle (Missy)

This past year has been filled with nothing but heartache and bad karma. It doesn't matter where I go, I think someone has figured out who I am. The news has stopped posting my pictures long ago, so I don't know how people keep figuring me out.

I'm in Prichard, Alabama right now. I had been hiding out here for the past three months but now I have to go.

"Please don't kill me." the maid begged.

See she saw me in the hallway the other day and looked at me twice, so she had to have figured me out right? Why else would she do a double take if she hadn't recognized me on the news for murder?

"If you didn't know who I was I wouldn't have to." I explained to her.

The only reason she was still alive is because I had to figure out how to kill her quietly. I didn't have any knives and I was too afraid to call for room service. I was scared that they would want to come all the way in. I've been staying at the Ritz Carlton thanks to this old white man I serviced. He got the room in his name for the next three days but when they find this house keeper dead, they will be calling him.

I made sure I was extra carefully coming and going because I always wore a fitted baseball cap. My hair had grown to shoulder length since I shaved my hair off, but I still didn't look like my old self. Hell, I even scratched off the skin on the tips of my fingers then burned them. Well Missy did that of course but we're one in the same.

I glanced around the room until the blow dryer caught my attention. I walked over to it and yanked it completely off the wall and approached the maid slowly. I had a sad expression on my face because I didn't want to kill her. I also didn't want to go to jail, so I had no other choice. I know if I tried to just leave Missy would come back and finish her off in a weird and unusual way.

"Please don't do this." she begged as I got within arm's reach. I lowered my head as I willed myself not to kill this woman. "I have children." she said as she tried to further plead her case.

That was all it took for me to walk out of the door. I left her tied to the chair because I knew housekeeping would come in and find her.

Missy (Michelle)

Sometimes I hate this weak bitch! That bitch probably doesn't even have kids! *"We'll see."* I thought to myself as I walked swiftly back into the room.

The maid's eyes filled with horror when she laid eyes on me again. I gave her a slight smirk as I walked up to her swiftly. I kicked her in the chest and knocked the chair completely over. I think the impact knocked the wind out of her because she was having a hard time catching her breath. I sat on my knees next to her as she had a coughing fit. I twisted my nose up in pure disgust once I got a whiff of her breath.

"Bitch your breath is being real disrespectful right now!" I snapped as I walked into the bathroom.

I needed to find something that smelled good. Everything was fucking bite size so I grabbed it all. "Open up." I said to her using my sing song voice. When I saw she wasn't going to open her mouth, I pinched her nose so she couldn't breathe. A few seconds later, she had no choice but to open her mouth. I squeezed all of the toothpaste in the back of her mouth.

She had no choice but to swallow it. I then opened up a bottle of shampoo and conditioner and poured them down her throat as well. She coughed and gagged. I jumped up right before she started to throw up. I stood there and watched her until she started choking. I allowed her to choke until I thought she was about to die. I turned the chair over on its side to help her out.

"You're not leaving me that easy sweetie." I said to her with a bright smile on my face. She didn't respond as she continued to throw up.

I waited patiently for her to finish then made my way back into the bathroom.

"Please no more." she begged. I smiled at her even though she couldn't see me.

I emptied the trash can, filled it up with water and grabbed a towel. I saw this shit on TV once and always wanted to do it. I was so hyped up about crossing this off of my bucket list that I almost dropped the water. I pulled my pants and panties off and sat on my knees behind her head.

I used my knees to lock her head in place then placed the towel on top of her face. I had no idea what the towel was going to do but I used it because they used it. I poured the water over the towel but it only took about five seconds before I ran out of water.

"Damn, I poured it too fast." I explained to her as I got up to fix more water.

When I returned, she was still coughing and choking. I shook my head at her as I tried it again. I laughed the entire time. Then a lightbulb went off! I hopped up and filled the trashcan with scorching hot water and came back. I removed the towel because I wanted to see what her skin would do. I could feel my pussy getting wet as I thought about the pain she was about to feel. I stood up because I didn't want to get burned when the water splattered. Hell, it was hard enough to hold this hot ass trash can.

I poured the water over her face slowly and she screamed out in pain. I watched her skin break away and roll off like little beads of rice. She continued to scream and I didn't want anyone to come save her. I stomped her head over and over until she stopped screaming. Hell even after she stopped screaming I kept stomping her. Blood was everywhere and now thanks to this bitch, I needed a shower! I went to the bathroom and took a quick shower, got dressed and headed out the room.

I walked all the way to the bus stop and paid this old lady to buy my tickets with money I stole from that old white man. "Atlanta are you ready for me?" I asked out loud.

Amere

I know something happened to Lisa, but I can't figure out exactly what it was. I had been halfway expecting her to be at the crib when I got out of the hospital last year, but she wasn't. I chalked it up to her not wanting to deal with my attitude after finding out Amiria was not my daughter. I actually only wanted to give my condolences. Had she made it, I would have still been in her life because I'm the only father she knew. Regardless of what those results said, she was my daughter. I helped raise her. I provided for her and her mother. For them to have a burial service and not make sure I was there was completely beyond me! I wanted to file a missing person's report on Lisa but shit, when she wants to be found I guess she will be. Anybody that runs off like she did deserves to get lost first. Trifling bitch.

As I scrolled through my contact list, I passed by Tamia's name. She and I have been keeping in contact as distant friends. She done packed up and moved to Atlanta and in all honesty, I'm trying to pull a Lisa on her ass. Remember how Lisa found out she lived in Detroit, so we moved out here? Yeah well that's what I've been thinking about doing this last month.

Tamia told me Armani has a son now and she named him Armad. I knew she only told me that to see if he was my child because Armani won't tell her who his dad is. Hell in all actuality, Armani probably doesn't know who his dad is. I'm sure she would tell Tamia if she knew. At first I was a little skeptical about keeping information that could hurt Tamia to myself, but it looks like Armani has turned over a new leaf.

Now I don't think Tamia and Rashard are doing good right now because these last few days she has answered every time I called her, and responded every time I texted her. I've tried to ask her what's going on with them, but not on no hating type shit. I want to know what's going on so I know if I can slide in somewhere. If Rashard is fucking up, I know Tamia will drop him like a bad habit; because that's how she did me. What makes him any different?

I've grown a lot and changed a lot and now I know my biggest mistake was ever cheating on a woman like Tamia. Then as if that wasn't bad enough, I cheated on her with a nothing ass bitch like Lisa. Now they're both Gone with the Wind.

I picked up my phone and called my cousin out in Atlanta.

"Yea?" He answered. I could tell he was trying to raise his voice over the loud music.

"Where you at fam?" I asked.

"You know Meech my nigga. I'm at the strip club. You here?" Meech asked and I wished like hell I was, but not to go to the strip club.

If I can get closer to Tamia, I can show her that I've changed. I just need a chance to show her I can be that man for her again.

"Not yet. I'm gone fly out this weekend but bruh." I said and paused because I really hate asking for shit. Niggas never let you live it down when you need them. They constantly bring up the fact that they had to help you.

"What's up?" He continued to yell over the music.

"My funds a lil dry. I need a job when I get there." I said and he agreed.

I know he's going to look out because we're family. Plus, he knows I can be trusted. Shit back on the coast, I was pretty hot shit. I wasn't running anything, but I was definitely well off. Everybody knew me, so everybody was willing to break bread with me. That's why I didn't want to move to Detroit. Shit for one, I didn't know anyone and people won't break bread with strangers. I've managed to do a little something around here lately, but I know it's because the streets have been dry. I don't know what happened around here but it's been a serious drought! I've been trying to find a connect, but I haven't had any luck. So really now, my best bet is to move out to Atlanta.

I only have $100,000 to my name and it may sound like a lot to you but shit, fast money goes faster. I knew I wouldn't be able to fly with this large sum of money, so I decided to make that 11-hour drive. I figured I'd go ahead and drive four hours now, then get a room and drive the rest of the way after check out. I packed a small bag and loaded my trunk with the money and my clothes. I pulled off, filled up my gas tank and headed to Atlanta.

Three hours in, I was beyond tired. Man I could barely keep my eyes open. I continued to drive another two hours and found one of those old motels. As I pulled in, it reminded me of the horror movie called Vacancy. The oddest thing was, the No flashed on and off just like it did on the movie. I parked and walked into the office. It was a small office with a large desk and one of those box TVs behind the desk. The TV had bunny ears on it that probably only allowed the skinny, white, snaggletooth clerk to see a couple of channels.

"Yea that movie had to have been shot here." I thought to myself as I approached the desk and cleared my throat. I paid for my room and he gave me a key that was hanging on a hook behind the desk.

All of these signs, you would think a nigga would dip out until I came to another one, but I was beyond tired. When I walked in my room, it smelled like stale cheese crackers and feet with a faint smell of cigarettes.

I looked around the room and took in the hard looking bed that I didn't want to sit on at all. The TV sat on the dresser but there were no drawers. "What the fuck kind of shit is this?" I asked myself out loud.

I turned the TV on but it wasn't working. That's when I saw the note on the wall. "Only 39.99 for antennas." I read out loud and shook my head. Oh these mufuckers trying to get over. I left back out the room, got a refund and left.

I drove until I came to a truck stop. I pulled in and took a nap. A few hours later I woke up, took a shower in the public restroom and left. Only a few more hours left to go and I'll be in Atlanta.

I shot Meech a text message to let him know how far out I was and he responded with an address. I guess that's where I'll be staying.

Armani

I had no earthly idea what to do after Tamia and Armad left. On one hand I was excited to have another break, but on the other hand, I didn't want Armad to get confused about who his mom was. Tamia spent more time with him than you know and I just don't want to be forgotten. It wouldn't be so bad if she spent the time with both of us. At least she's not teaching him to call her mommy. She tells him that he's Tt's big boy.

They had been gone well into the night and I figured I'd get out on the town. I haven't had the chance to experience the night life here yet, so why not get out now. I drew me a hot bath and poured my bath beads inside. As I stripped all of my clothes off, I stared at myself with pure disgust. Tamia was right, I do need to join a gym or something. Sure I just had a baby but damn, I had done let myself go. My hair wasn't even done and that's not like me at all! I shook my head as I slid my body in the hot water. I laid completely still as I let the hot water caress my body.

I could hear my phone ringing but I refused to get up and answer it. I couldn't help but wish that Tamia and I were friends because maybe then, she and I could go out together. I could find a sixteen year-old and pay her to keep Armad.

First thing first, I need to find a job. The only thing I know how to do is fuck and twerk so I'm going to have to go to a strip club. I kind of wanted to go to school, but I don't know if I will have help with Armad or not. It's so stressful to try to be a mother and still have a life. Thank God for Tamia and Rashard because they do everything for us. I haven't had to buy a single thing! Not that I would have the money to do so anyway, but still.

My phone started ringing as thoughts of me being broke filled my mind again. I climbed out of the tub and made my way to my phone without drying off. I left a trail of water all the way to the kitchen and back in the bathroom. I slid my finger across the screen to answer without looking at the phone.

"Damn I knew you missed daddy!" Dave said with a lust filled voice.

I frowned my face up and held my phone up to take him off of speaker phone when I realized he was Facetiming me. As soon as our eyes connected, the frown went away from my face. All those "I've changed" thoughts left my mind. He was still as sexy as he was the last time I seen him.

I didn't respond to his statement. I stepped into the tub and held my IPhone high to give him a full view of my body. My clit started to tingle as he lowered the phone down to his lap. I could see his hard dick straining against his zipper as it tried to break free. Dave sat the phone down and I groaned loudly. When he picked it back up, I saw my favorite guy. Out of all of my sex partners and baby I've lost count, Dave is the most memorable. I don't want to say he's the best I've ever had because I can't be too sure.

Dave and Amere are kind of neck to neck when it comes to being the best. They both have great head and awesome dick, but they lay the pipe in two different ways. Dave is always really aggressive. He slaps my ass cheeks, pulls my hair and slams into me. Then I have Amere who's gentle with me. He grinds in the pussy. I cum like crazy with both of them, so I can't really say which one is the best. If I could fuck both of them I would. My clit jumped at the thought of how they both handled me in the past.

My mouth watered as I watched Dave stroke his long, thick dick slowly. I licked my lips as I slid my hand down to my clit. I used my index and ring finger to my part lips as I inserted my middle finger slowly. I moaned softly as I tilted my head back against the back of the tub. I glanced at the screen lustfully and noticed Dave was watching me. He moaned out as well. I turned my phone so he could get a good view of what I was doing to myself.

"Where are you?" Dave asked with a husky voice.

I stopped what I was doing with an aggravated expression on my face. Shit I was just about to get off and he want to distract me. I hadn't had a nut in 6 months!

"I'm home!" I said as I sighed dramatically. My water had gotten cold and my nut was gone. I let the water out of the tub and climbed out.

"I want you." Dave said. I just stared at the phone with a stupid expression on my face.

"Nigga!" I said clearly frustrated.

I did not want to have one of those "who wants who" the most conversations right now. Maybe if he had let me catch my nut, I'd be a bit nicer.

"I'm in Atlanta." He said calmly. My eyes got as big and as round as saucers as I looked at his serious facial expression.

I quickly gave him my address and hung up the phone. "No need to go out when the party is coming to me!" I cheered as I dried my body off.

I had stretch marks on my stomach from being pregnant and they looked horrible! I know Dave is used to me blemish free, so I started to get nervous. "Damn I gotta get myself together." I said out loud. I lotioned my body and sprayed a few squirts of Amber Romance from Victoria's Secret. It was my all-time favorite scent because it's soft and subtle, yet it lasts.

Once I was done, I slipped on my sheer robe, a pair of heels I brought with me from Detroit and made my way to the living room. I desperately needed to calm my nerves for a night I'm sure I'd never forget.

Tamia

Armad and I ran the streets all day long. We went grocery shopping together then back home to put the groceries away. Then we went for a stroll on the beach. My mind was so preoccupied with him that I hadn't realized that I hadn't talked to my man all day. I shrugged it off as I loaded Armad in his seat so we could go home. There wasn't much I needed from Armani because he had just as much stuff at my house as he did hers.

When we got home, I gave him a bath, fed him and put him down to sleep. I turned the digital baby monitor on so I could see him and hear him from the other room. I was completely drained and had no energy to call and fuss with Rashard for his lack of efforts today. The only thing I wanted to do was take a shower and fix me something simple to eat since I would more than likely be eating alone.

After my shower, I walked slowly through our new home. It was bigger and more beautiful than the last house he bought me, but what's the point? We are hardly ever home and when I am here, I'm alone. I shook my head as I passed by a picture of us laughing. I remember the day of the photo shoot like it was yesterday.

"Baby why you want to take professional pictures?" Rashard asked as we got dressed. He was going to wear a turquoise polo shirt and jeans. I matched him by wearing a turquoise maxi dress.

"So we can hang them on the wall dummy." I said with a smirk on my face. He mimicked me as he walked up behind me and placed his arms around my waist. I moaned out as he sucked softly on my neck. "Baby we gotta go." I said lustfully as I tried to sidestep out of his embrace.

He stepped to the side with me and continued to hold me close.

"I love you." He said and it shocked my soul! He had never said that to me before.

I didn't know what to say back. Hell, I wasn't even sure if I felt love or lust. I turned around to face him and kissed him on his lips.

"Oh yea?" I asked as I looked into his eyes. He squeezed my ass cheeks and pulled me closer as he nodded his head. "If I was dating all of this." I paused as I gestured to my body. "I'd love me too." I continued and walked out of the door.

Rashard slapped me on the ass as he followed me out of the house. He shocked me again when he opened the passenger's side door for me. "Another bitch better not be pregnant." I thought to myself. I shook my head of the negative thoughts as I watched him walk around to the driver's side of the car. He hopped in and we made it there in less than fifteen minutes.

I followed him inside of the building and we were shown to the room we would be taking pictures in. The photographer instructed us to relax and just have fun as he did his thing.

He took several pictures of us then turned the radio on. "She Got a Donk" remix by Nicki Minaj came blaring through the speakers. I instantly bent over and started bouncing my booty up and down. I halfway expected Rashard to start dancing too but he was in a trance. He walked up behind me and slid his arms around me. I stood up straight with a smile on my face as I continued to dance.

"You tryna get fucked right here?" Rashard asked with a serious expression on his face. I laughed and took a step forward. Rashard pulled me back to him roughly. "You feel him?" He asked as he positioned himself directly behind me.

"Yea." I said then turned around to face him. I threw my arms around his neck and kissed him passionately. "I'm going to take you behind that curtain and suck the skin off your dick." I said loud enough for him to hear me over the music but not loud enough for the photographer to hear.

"Oh yeah?" He asked with his eyes big. I nodded my head and turned back around. "Right now?" He asked and I nodded my head. He grabbed my hand and pulled me in the direction of the curtain.

"Bay?" I called out as I stopped him from pulling me. He stopped and looked at me with eyes

filled with lust. "Got em!" I screamed then fell out laughing.
He scooped me up his arms as I laughed. He kissed my cheek and joined in on the laughter.

I continued to stare at the picture of us. It was my all-time favorite picture, but it wasn't real. Sure enough the moment was real but this picture isn't us. The smile on my face in the picture hasn't been there in a long time. Hell, we haven't even spent time together in a long time. I kind of want to fix our relationship, but I kind of want to just leave.

Rashard

I walked in the house and the smell of fried chicken invaded my nostrils. I closed my eyes and inhaled deeply as I followed the smell to the kitchen.

"What you cooking baby?" I asked as I took a seat at the counter. We had one of those island counters in the middle of the kitchen with three bar stools.

"Breaded chicken tenders, homemade macaroni and string beans." She said to me.

I noticed her voice wasn't laced with an attitude but she also didn't turn around to talk to me.

She continued to busy herself at the stove, so I knew something was wrong. I wanted to wrap my arms around her to let her know I'm here, but I didn't want her to want to fuck. A nigga was drained out from fucking with Natasia all damn day. I knew I hadn't fucked Tamia in about three days though, so I know if I touched her, she will want some dick.

"You good?" I asked with an eyebrow raised. I held my breath as I waited for her to answer. It felt like she was taking forever to nod her damn head but she did. That let me know that she wasn't good.

I had no choice but to walk up to her. I sent a silent prayer up that she wouldn't want to fuck, because I don't even know if my dick will stand up again today. Well at least not for the next two hours.

"Talk to me." I said as I wrapped my arms around her body tightly.

She normally melted in my arms but this time, I felt her body tense up. I looked at her suspiciously because I know she ain't know shit about what I was doing, so now I'm wondering what the fuck she been doing. I stared at her as I thought about why we haven't had sex in a couple of days. *"This bitch hasn't tried to give me no pussy!"* I thought to myself as I frowned my face up at her.

I raised her shirt up so I could slide my hand in her panties to do a pussy check. I needed to stick my finger in it to see if the shit was three days tight or if she had some this morning.

She grabbed my wrist tightly and flung my hand away from her. She looked up at me with a look of disgust on her face. Like I, Rashard mother fucking Peterson disgusts her! I don't disgust no fucking body.

"What's yo problem?!" I asked. I was beyond pissed that she didn't let me touch what was supposed to had been my pussy.

"Armad here." She said.

"Who gives a flying fuck T? He's a baby! He not in here and if he was, he can't see shit but shapes right now!" I snapped at her. I couldn't believe she was coming at me with that bullshit ass reason!

I didn't want to fuck her anyway but that's beside the point! Since Tamia and I started fucking, she has never turned down the dick! Shit, this meat is what's been keeping us together!

She pissed me off even more when she rolled her eyes and shook her head at me. She didn't even respond to what I had said to her. I shook my head as I fought with myself. I needed to make sure I didn't knock her little ass backwards because that's exactly what I wanted to do.

"Keep being a hoe and you gone be a homeless hoe!" I snapped and walked out of the room.

I opened the front door then realized how wrong I was for saying that to her. I slammed the door shut and made my way back into the kitchen quietly.

I stood in the entrance and watched her finish preparing her meal like what just happened hadn't even affected her. That let me know that she's doing her own thing. Two can play that game though.

I left out of the house, hopped in my car and burned rubber on my way out of the driveway. "I ain't got time for a bitch I can't trust!" I said out loud to myself. I turned the radio on and began to jam. Chris Brown and Lil Wayne was right on time with this hit.

I wasn't born last night
I know these hoes ain't right
But you was blowing up her phone last night
But she ain't have her ringer nor her ring on last night, oh
Nigga, that's that nerve
Why give a bitch your heart
When she rather have a purse?
Why give a bitch an inch
When she rather have nine?
You know how the game goes
She'll be mine by half time, I'm the shit, oh
Nigga, that's that nerve
You all about her and she's all about hers
Birdman junior in this bitch, no flamingo
And I done did everything but trust these hoes

I bobbed my head to the beat because these hoes really ain't loyal! I bought the bitch not one but two houses! I bought her back stabbing ass best friend a condo and I take care of both of them bitches and what she do? Go hop in the next nigga's bed. It's cool though.

I made my way downtown to the Diamonds of Atlanta strip club. Man, it be some bad bitches in there! People think Magic City is the hottest but they're sleeping on these diamonds.

I pulled up in the parking lot and got out of my ride. I made my way casually through the doors.

Every time I walk in it's like my first time. The inside of the club has a jaw dropping theme every time you enter it. They have all black leather reclining chairs and all black leather sectionals. Then the stage! Man the stage got so many poles on it, I don't know which bitch I should make it rain on! There isn't a single clock anywhere that I could see and I know exactly why they did it. They want you to come in and lose track of time. Shit by the time you leave, you won't have a clue what time it was or how much money you spent.

I made my way to get singles and then walked around until I spotted Meech. I walked up to his VIP section and dapped everybody up that were sitting there.

"Aye lemme holla at you fam." Meech said. He signaled for the chicks that were sitting on both sides of him to get up. I could tell they had an attitude about being sent on their way, but it was time to talk business. Whenever it was time to talk business, the hoes had to go.

"What's up?" I asked once they were out of the section.

He poured himself a shot so I took that time to study my surroundings. I hadn't really been out since we've been here since, I've been either at home or Natasia's house.

We were in the VIP section alone with the exception of two body guards that stood at the entrance to prevent anyone from entering without permission. They were big, bulky niggas too and one of them had a fade with a tail in the back. That bitch was long as fuck too. I shook my head and scanned the crowd. I noticed a pack of over the top niggas that stood in front of the stage. They caught my attention because they weren't throwing any money. One of them was kind of off to side. I quickly looked away when his eyes traveled to this VIP section. I instantly knew something was about to go down, but I didn't know what. I left my piece in the car so I was in this bitch naked, about to get caught up in some shit I don't have shit to do with.

"My cousin on his way down here. I'm gone put him on. He used to do his thang on the coast but he fell off after he moved." Meech said to me. I just nodded my head because I don't know why I needed to know that shit.

Meech is the boss of his crew and it feel like he's running shit by me right now.

"It's your call." I said as I looked back out at the crowd.

"You think it's a smart move?" Meech asked.

That is the reason why he hasn't been able to take over Atlanta. When you running shit, you don't look to the next mufucker to tell you what kind of moves you're making.

"I don't know buddy, you do. Ask yourself that." I said without looking at him.

The guys had begun to split up.

"Aye you know them?" I asked and pointed in their direction.

I looked at Meech and his ass poured another shot first. By the time he looked up, they were no longer together.

"Who?" He asked as he stood up.

He staggered slightly and I knew he had past his drinking limit twice. They were about to catch my boy slipping and it was nothing I could do about it. I shook my head as I continued to scan the crowd. One of them was by the front door, two were by the bathroom door and the other sat off to side. He was staring unwaveringly at the VIP section. I refused to look directly at him because I didn't want them to know that I was on to them.

"You packing?" I asked Meech as he sat down.

He nodded his head. I held my hand out and the nigga gave it to me with no questions asked. I shook my head as I concealed the weapon.

"Aye, let's get outta here fam." I said as I stood to my feet.

Meech staggered slightly as he stood to his feet. I walked ahead of him and told the security guards to escort him to his ride.

I caught a bad vibe from them but I know how hard it is for me to trust a mufucker. In this case, in this moment, at this time, I didn't trust a soul in my presence. All I know is, I need to get my boy the fuck out of dodge before shit pops off. One of the guards nodded his head and helped Meech down the stairs. I allowed my eyes to roam the crowd and noticed they were all watching us. I kept walking behind the guard that was helping Meech until I felt a presence behind me. I glanced back and the guard with the tail was following closely behind us.

We made it out of the door just as gunfire rang out.

Michelle

The bus ride from Alabama to Atlanta was the longest, most uncomfortable ride of my life! I lost count of how many times we got off and got back on. Ain't nobody got time for that shit! There was this one lady that kept looking at me but I hadn't had a chance to get near her. I wasn't going to kill her, I just wanted to ask her if she knew me from somewhere or if I had done something to her. We had one more stop to make and I was just going to follow her to where ever she was going so we could talk in private.

Rashard walked through doors and I couldn't explain the feeling I got every time I saw him. My heart filled with love and my panties filled with juices. It was always like that when I saw him because we belong together. All of that faded away when Tamia emerged from the crowd. We were at Deuce's birthday party at Carte Blanche and Tamia was hosting it. Normally Candy was the only person Raph allowed to host, so I don't know why they chose Tamia.

I walked right up to Rashard and didn't think he and Tamia had anything going on until I reached him.

"I got a girl now. The host. Respect her and get the fuck outta my face." Rashard leaned over and whispered in my ear.

When I looked up into his eyes, they were black. I didn't understand. We were just together Saturday when I twisted his dreads. I turned around and stormed away.

"Sweetie we're here." A female voice said as my body shook.

When I opened my eyes, I realized I had fallen asleep. Anger swept through my body as I thought about the dream I had. I hadn't dreamed of that night since I left Detroit so why now?

"Thank you." I said to the lady as I stood to my feet. I scanned the seats and shook my head. The lady was gone. *"I hope she didn't recognize you!"* Missy said with an attitude. I shook my head again and made my way off the bus.

I walked around the bus station and still couldn't find the lady. I gave up and just started walking. I didn't know where I was going but I was going to get there. I watched the people around me as I walked through the dangerous streets of Atlanta. I made sure I was able to see their faces without showing them my face. I know that if I hadn't left Detroit, I could have faced those charges and won but I would have to sit in jail until then.

"Hey do you need a ride?" I heard someone ask.

When I looked towards the voice, a slow smile began to spread across my face. It was the lady that had been watching me on the bus. I looked around cautiously to make sure nobody saw us talking. I approached the car slowly and glanced inside. There was a man driving and she was in the back seat. *"Oh she must be hot stuff!"* I thought to myself.

"Don't worry he won't bite." She said with a smile after she noticed me look at him. I for damn sure didn't mind that sexy beast of a man biting me at all! I will most definitely turn around and give him something to bite!

"I um, I don't have a destination." I said upfront.

If I hopped in knowing good and well that I didn't have anywhere to go, I would no doubt have to kill her and the guy. I'm not even experienced in killing yet. I mean I have a few nice kills on my resume but shit, it would take a lot to kill his big ass.

"How about you come to my place?" She asked and shocked the fuck out of me. I was beyond confused because she doesn't know me. She was watching me on the bus now she wants to take me home like I'm a puppy or something.

"Are you the police? If you are, you have to tell me." I said because I needed to run if she was. Ain't nobody have time to be killing cops and shit, but I will if I have to. She chuckled lightly.

"Sweetie you know that's not true don't you?" She asked. I gave her a shoulder shrug. I know I heard that shit before but oh well. "If you have done something that will make the police come after you and if I was the police, you would have been arrested after you stepped off of the bus sweetheart." She said as she looked directly at me. It made total sense.

I released a breath I didn't know I was holding. I nodded my head and walked around to the other side of the car and hopped in.

"What's your name?" She asked. I stared ahead without responding to her question. I looked out the window then back at her. "If you don't want to tell me your real name, make one up. Make it good because you won't be able to change it." She said to me.

I could feel her eyes burning a hole in the side of my head.

"Missy." I answered.

When I heard a chuckle, I looked at the lady then the guy but they both had serious expressions on their faces. I knew the only other person it could have come from was Missy.

"Shit is about to get real." I thought to myself as I closed my eyes.

<u>Amere</u>

When I made it to Atlanta, I gave Meech a call but he didn't answer his phone. I shook my head and looked for the address he gave me. Once I found it, I entered it into my navigation app on my phone.

It took about 20 minutes for me to pull up to the address. It was a nice size navy blue brick house. I cut the car off and made my way up to the door. I knocked and waited for someone to answer. I turned around so I could scope the neighborhood out. It seemed like a nice quiet neighborhood but being raised where I was raised, I know looks can be deceiving.

"Who is it?" I heard a female voice ask.
"Amere." I answered as I turned sideways. I wanted to be able to see who answered the door as well as make sure nobody was going to sneak up on me.

The door swung open and this beautiful chick stood before me with a frown on her face. She had shoulder length jet black hair with a mole underneath her right eye. I allowed my eyes to scan the rest of her toned body. She was wearing a sports bra and tights with the running shoes to match. If I had to guess, I had interrupted her workout. I noticed there was a small amount of sweat on her stomach when my eyes landed on the sexiest belly button ring I had ever seen in my life. The belly button ring had a studded diamond at the top but a naked woman dangled under it. I licked my lips and continued to allow my eyes to roam the rest of her body. That camel toe was nothing to play with! I wanted to get down and nibble on it through her tights.

She cleared her throat and I looked back up at her apologetically. I was simply admiring a beautiful woman.

"You gone come in or just stare at me all damn day? I was busy." She said then walked away from the door.

I looked behind me because this has got to be some type of trick. Maybe even a set up. I pulled my phone out of my pocket and called Meech back but he didn't answer. I threw all caution to the side and walked inside of the house.

It was really clean and decorated nicely, so I could tell this is her home. I walked into the living room, it was where she walked off to and saw she had started her work out backup. There was some guy on the screen having them do shit that I know would kill me, yet she was doing it like it was nothing. I watched her until he gave her a break. She grabbed a bottle of water off the table and turned to face me.

"I'll show you around after I finish. I have six minutes left." She said then turned around without giving me a chance to respond.

My eyes scanned the living room until they landed on the DVD case of the workout video she was doing, *Insanity*. *"That's exactly what it is."* I thought to myself as I watched her do her thing for next six minutes.

When she was done, she stretched then turned the TV completely off. She took another swig of water then turned to face me.

"Sorry about that. I really just don't like getting interrupted. It's too hard to jump back in the swing of things that way." She explained.

I nodded my head because I guess I can understand that. Not to mention, if I'm going to be staying here, I don't want to get off on the wrong foot.

"Ok c'mon." she said as she threw her towel over her shoulder.

I followed her a short distance and she showed me the kitchen. She walked off and pointed at two guest rooms and the hall bathroom. When we got to the back of the house, she showed me my room and told me her room was the last door around the corner. I nodded my head and turned to go in my room. The room was a nice sized room. Well shit, it was a nice sized house. I opened the drawer and placed my few belongings in them and walked in the bathroom to take a shower.

After my shower, I walked in the living room but she wasn't there. I wanted to call out to her but I realized I didn't know what the fuck her name was. I shook my head and made my way back inside my room. I was beyond tired after that ride plus I knew that shower and this bed was exactly what I needed.

Armani

Dave made my body feel so good last night that I got up and cooked the nigga breakfast. Ok I'm lying, but I wanted to. Shit you know I can't cook. I probably could if I actually tried but I've never had to. Growing up without food I was always hungry, so I would sneak to Tamia's house and eat or just eat at school. Then we moved to Detroit together and she always cooked, so I never had to learn. Even now, she will cook and ask me if I want some and bring me a plate. Whenever she doesn't ask, I just go get something to eat.

I actually got up to start breakfast but I got aggravated because I kept burning the bacon. I cooked the eggs first without thinking they would get cold before the bacon was ready. Shit, I had to throw it all in the trash. I washed the dishes and put them up like I had never been in the kitchen at all. I didn't know how long Dave would be here, but he was going to treat me to breakfast and probably some dick before he left.

When I opened my room door, Dave was sound asleep. I crawled underneath the covers from the foot of the bed and made my way to his hard dick. I smiled to myself because I knew he would be rock hard because they all are in the mornings. I sucked the tip of it into my mouth without using my hands as I sucked aggressively at his head. I continued to tease him until I felt him thrust his hips forward slightly. That let me know that he was awake and ready for me.

I pulled his long dick out of my mouth and spit on it to make it nice and wet. Dave loves sloppy head. If you ever want to make his ass squeal like a pig and run from you, make it sloppy. The sloppier the better. I used both hands to jerk him off as I placed the tip back in my mouth. I bobbed my head on the tip until I got in a good rhythm. I removed one hand so I could allow him to go deeper into my warm mouth. I began to hum the tune of Ms. Mary Mack as I continued to bob up and down on his dick. He moaned and met my head movements with his hips. That let me know I wasn't in control. I didn't like that shit at all! I sucked harder as I stroked him with one hand. He moaned out and thrust into my mouth again. I heard his toes pop and that meant he was curling them. *"This is my chance."* I thought to myself.

I cuffed his balls in one hand and applied just a little bit of pressure to them. I sucked up and down his shaft slowly. Each time, I took him further down my throat.

"Shit." he moaned out as he placed his hand on my head. He tried to push my face away so I sucked harder. "Shit! Baby hold on." He moaned out in a raspy voice. I sucked harder and relaxed my throat muscles so I could take him deeper. "Ah fuck!" He screamed out as his legs tensed up then went weak like noodles. I smiled on the inside as I continued to drain him of his seeds. I swallowed and headed straight to the bathroom.

I brushed my teeth and tongue then gargled with mouthwash before I felt clean again. I have no idea why I always swallow when I hate how it feels going down. I bet I have a stomach filled with cum after last night's head session.

When I made my way back in the room, this nigga was still laying down. Shit, this nigga looked even more comfortable than he did before I gave him some morning head. I shook my head and made my way to the side of the bed.

"Get up Daddy!" I said as I snatched the cover completely off the bed. I smiled at the face he made as he balled his body up.

"Why baby? Just let me sleep a little longer." He said with his eyes still closed.

"No I'm hungry. Get up and get dressed." I replied calmly.

He sat up slowly and grabbed his pants off the floor. I watched him cautiously as he dug his hand deep in his pocket and pulled out a wad of cash. I hadn't gotten paid for my services in so long that I didn't know how to react to all of this money. I didn't sleep with him for something in return this time but I wasn't about to turn down no money either. I walked away and placed the wad of money in a shoebox inside of my closet. It's time to get my sponsors back up so I won't need Tamia and Rashard anymore. I'll be able to move about how I want. Hell if I need to, I can get Tamia to watch Armad while I go out and scope my next victim.

When I returned back to the bed, Dave was attempting to lay back down.

"I think you misunderstood what was about to happen." I said as I pulled the covers off of him again. He let out a frustrated groan as he turned around to look at me. His phone started to ring on the nightstand. We both looked at it at the same time.

"Wifey. Hmm." I said then sucked my teeth. I rolled my eyes, folded my arms across my chest and waited for Dave to explain. "Why the fuck are you here?" I asked calmly.

This was like the calm before the storm because I done let this nigga back in. He got me open and ready to hop back on my hoe stroll because that's all I know how to do.

"I came for you." He said as his phone finally stopped ringing.

"For me?" I asked with a confused look on my face. I couldn't for the life of me, understand why this man has been blowing me up since I left when he's still married.

"Yes baby. We're getting a divorce." He said as he looked directly in my face.

I walked up close to him with a smile on my face. There is no way he would be able to make direct eye contact and lie through his teeth. Right? Wrong! *Whap!* I hit Dave so hard across his face that his body twisted and almost fell off the bed.

"I deserved that." He said just as his phone started to ring again.

"Just get out." I said as I shook my head. All I wanted was some dick and breakfast and he just fucked that up for me.

"Baby." he called out as he stood to his feet. He tried to grab me but I stepped out of his reach and snatched the sheets off the bed. I needed to wash all of this shit to get his scent out of here. I was going to do shit different this time around. Nobody would know where my son and I lay our heads. I know how unsafe that shit is now. I know how easy it is to make these memories in your home. Now I know how hard it is to get rid of them.

I stuffed the linen into my washing machine aggressively. I couldn't tell if I was more mad at him or myself. I was doing so fucking good alone. I wasn't messing around with anyone and I didn't feel any type of way. In the blink of an eye, he walked in and destroyed my peace. I was focused. Now I'm, man I don't even fucking know what to call it right now.

"It's not what you think." I heard Dave say.

I looked towards the sound of his voice and couldn't believe he was standing in the doorway fully dressed.

"Oh yea?" I asked then chuckled lightly to myself. I don't really know how I should feel right now. All I do know is, I wish I never answered for him last night.

"We are getting a divorce." He said again as he stared at me. "I want to be with you." He continued. I could hear the plea in his voice and it almost softened my heart.

When I looked at him again I saw red. I attacked him and landed blows wherever he wasn't blocking them.

"Chill out!" He screamed in my face but that didn't stop me. He slammed into the wall and that made me fight harder.

He wrapped his arms around me and squeezed until I wasn't swinging anymore. I tried to break free but I couldn't. I was trapped. I will forever be this person that everyone hates because I cannot break free. I stood there in Dave's arms wondering why I couldn't change.

I wondered how I ever got to this point. How did I ever allow myself to turn on the one person that would have had my back forever? I didn't know what to do anymore. It was so easy just being me, but it wasn't easy hurting Tamia. I began to realize that I was just jealous of her life. It wasn't even that her life was better than mines, because she had it rough too. I was jealous because she made it out with her brains and I merely rode her coattail because I could. I was jealous because she has been through a lot yet you can't tell by looking at her or her actions. She moves like a bitch that was born with a silver spoon in her mouth.

Fresh tears stung my eyes as a lump formed in the back of my throat. I laid my head on Dave's chest as I cried loudly. He held me tighter and my body went limp in his arms. He lifted my body and carried me back into my room. He laid me on my bare bed and took my clothes off slowly. That wasn't something that I wanted him to do. I wanted him to leave and go back home to his wife. I wanted him to go back to Detroit and never come back again. Yes, that's what I wanted him to do. This is what I needed at this moment. An escape. Even if only just for this moment. I needed to feel loved. I needed to feel wanted. Even if it was all just a game. Even if it was all just a plot to get back between my legs. A ploy to make me his side chick again.

I looked down and moaned softly as Dave sucked my clit with his finger in my pussy. I circled my hips as I fucked his mouth and finger at the same time. He sucked harder and I continued to grind on his face. I could feel a powerfully orgasm coming so I did not stop moving. I continued to grind until my body began to tremble. Dave gripped me tight as he sucked harder and harder. If I wasn't mistaken, I'd swear he sucked my soul completely out of my body. My body went limp.

Dave's phone started to ring again. This time it was a text message. I glanced at his phone and saw that it was his wife again. He climbed out of bed and read the message. I turned over on my side.

"Baby." he called out to me.

"Just go." I said. He didn't put up a fight this time. He just left. This is my life.

Tamia

The nerve of that nigga to come in here questioning me. That man was gone all day yesterday and came back smelling like Dove! I don't even fucking buy Dove for the house so whatever bitch he was with does. I promise one thing; I don't have time for this bullshit. I was supposed to work today but I know that after I'm done doing what I need to do, I'll be tired. See I've never snapped on Rashard and I've honestly been trying not to. I think he's mistaken my lack of snapping out for something else though. I'm not afraid of losing him because I know what's for me will always be for me. What I'm not going to do is sit around and wait for someone to decide if they're for me or not.

I really couldn't believe the audacity of him to accuse me of cheating! I literally go to work and come back home. The only time I'm gone and not at either place is when I'm spending the day with Armad. Speaking of him, I need to get him home to his mother but I need to pack me a bag first. I'm going to see if I can stay with Armani until I find a place of my own. One thing Rashard will never do again is threaten to put me out. He's about to find out what it's like to live in this big ass empty house alone. Well maybe not, since he's the one that's never here.

I strapped Armad down in his car seat then carried our belongings out to the car. I shook my head as I walked back inside to get Armad. "Bitch ass nigga didn't even come home last night." I said out loud to myself.

Once he was all strapped in the car seat, we headed to Armani's house. I grabbed Armad and headed to the door. I knocked softly at first but she didn't come to the door. I knocked a little bit harder and she still didn't come to the door. I checked the time on my phone and it was almost ten so I knew she should be awake. Her car was in the driveway so I know she's home. I got worried so I started banging on the door.

"Hey what's going on?!" A disgruntled neighbor from down the hall came and asked.

"Have you seen her leave?" I asked with worry evident in my voice. I could tell from the way his features softened that he knew I was worried. He shook his head and approached me. After all the shit I've been through and seen, I took a cautious step back. Hell for all I know, he could have killed Armani and was waiting on me to come here for whatever reason, so he could kill me too. I picked the car seat up and took another step away from him. He held his hands up and stopped in his tracks once he realized I was afraid of him.

"I'm not going to hurt you." He said then took a step back. He kept his hands in the air. I turned back towards the door and started banging on it again.

"MANI!!!" I yelled. "Fuck I hope she's ok." I thought to myself as I continued to knock on the door.

When I looked back at the neighbor, he was still standing there like he wanted to see what would happen as well. I continued to bang on the door. This was once my best friend and although I don't trust her, I don't want any harm to come to her. I used my phone to call her but she didn't answer. I turned my back to the door and sighed. I could feel a lump forming in my throat as I sent a silent prayer up. I needed her to be ok. Hell Armad needed her to be ok.

I leaned against the door just as the tears began to fall. I fell inside of her condo because she opened the door just as I leaned against it.

"Ouch!" I yelled out as I grimaced in pain. "What the fuck is going on?" Armani asked with an attitude. When I looked back and saw her, I jumped up and gave her a super tight hug.

"Girl what the hell wrong with you?" She asked as she shoved me off of her lightly.

I looked at her disheveled appearance and my jaw hit the floor. Her hair was all over her head. The only thing she had on was a sheer robe and it was wide open. She had a deep frown etched on her face with a trail of dried saliva that started at the corner of her mouth and stopped right by her ear.

"Are you ok?" I asked as I frowned at her. I forgot the neighbor was standing there until Armani's eyes looked past me. I turned around and looked and noticed he was just standing there staring at her.

I grabbed Armad's seat and pushed my way past her into the house. I looked down at him and couldn't believe he slept through all of that. I walked straight into the living room.

"Why were you banging on my door like something was wrong with you?!" Armani asked as she placed her hand on her hip. I took notice of the hickey on her neck but I didn't say a thing. It's not my place. We aren't really friends anyway.

"I thought something was wrong with you." I said softly.

I know I miss the friendship we had before I found out about Amere but I don't know if it's attainable anymore. I think if we tried, I'd always think in the back of my mind that she wants whoever I'm with.

"Naw I'm good." She replied and walked off. I took Armad out of his seat and laid him in his crib. He's such a good baby. The only time he cries is when he needs his diaper changed or when he's hungry.

After I made sure he went back to sleep, I went on a search to find Armani. She was back in her bed. As many times as I've been here, her bed is always made so I know something is wrong with her.

"Get up." I said as I tapped her foot. She snatched her foot out of my reach. "Get up Mani!" I said with a little more bass in my voice.

I think it's about time I get my friend back. I grabbed her ankle with both hands and pulled her to the end of the bed with all of my might. "Get up!" I yelled. She sat up and swung but she missed. I was shocked but this was well overdue.

I took a step back so she could get up. We both knew what was about to happen. Growing up on the coast, when you had a problem with someone that couldn't be talked out, you duked it out. These days, people are either scared of getting beat up or just can't fight so they shoot. If we took to that kind of thinking, one of us would have to die. Especially with all the bullshit that has surrounded us. Hell I don't even know what her problem ever was with me.

"What's your problem?" I asked just as I swung and hit her in the jaw.

She did a little two step from the impact of my blow but sent two blows to my stomach. I doubled over in pain as I looked up at her.

"You think you're better than me." She said then punched me in my jaw. The blow sent me flying down to my knees in confusion.

"No Armani." I paused. "You think I'm better than you!" I snapped then spit blood out of my mouth.

I stood back up to my feet. I noticed she was taken aback by my words, but they were the truth. I had never said or done anything to imply that I was better than her. Those were thoughts that she put in her head on her own.

I rushed her. We both hit the bed and flipped over the other side of it. I punched her three times in the face.

"Why'd you fuck Amere?" I asked. She used her body to push me off of her and I hit my head on her night stand.

I felt dazed as I sat next to it. I touched the spot and looked at my fingers. I shook my head because I was bleeding. When I looked at Armani, she looked worried about me. It was probably from the amount of blood that was pouring out my wound. I dove at her and sent more blows to her face and stomach. "Why'd you fuck him?" I asked because I really needed to know. I continued to hit her as tears fell down her cheeks. I continued to swing until I got tired.

"I'm sorry." She cried out. Almost instantly, all the built up anger I had inside was gone. This is what I had been waiting on and I had no idea. "I just wanted someone to love me the way he loved you." She continued.

I climbed off of her and sat on the floor next to her. She sat up slowly but continued to cry. She had a busted lip and her nose was bleeding.

"I miss you." I finally admitted. She cried harder and reached out to hug me.

Armad started to cry and it snapped us both out of our moment.

Rashard

POW! POW! POW! Bullets whizzed by our heads as we all ducked and took cover. I saw the body guard that was helping Meech drop him and jump behind a van. I shook my head as I took a look behind us. The sound of gunfire could still be heard but I didn't see any shooters. Strangely, I didn't see the bodyguard with the tail either. I wanted to get my boy out of dodge but I wasn't about to get shot trying to save his life. Shit he knows that if he's trying to take shit over, he needs to be on his P's and Q's at all times. That way, he will never get caught slipping like this. I turned my attention back to Meech briefly. He was attempting to stand to his feet in the middle of gunfire. I shook my head at his drunken carelessness.

Then it was like time stood still except for the people involved in the immediate gun battle. I could hear the faint sound of someone screaming in the distance. The other body guard suddenly appeared from the other side of the parking lot. I briefly wondered how he got over there so quickly. I watched as he made his way to Meech who staggered through the parking lot. It was as if Meech was completely unaware of his surroundings. Now I've seen niggas drunk but one thing I've learned about drunk niggas is they sober up quick when their life's in danger and when the police is near. This man has been drugged. I got up slowly and made my way around the opposite end of the truck that I was crouched down behind. I stayed low so the bodyguard wouldn't see me. I made eye contact with the other bodyguard just as he took two bullets to his chest. I shook my head as I watched him drop like a sack of hammers.

The sound of more gunfire caused me to look in the direction of the club. I saw what looked like a pile of bodies in front of the entrance. I shook my head because of the innocent lives lost due to pure fuckery. I continued making my way to Meech as I watched my surroundings. He stumbled into a nearby car.

"Aye playa where ya car at?" I heard the bodyguard ask. Meech responded inaudibly. The body guard raised his gun to Meech's head.

"Say playa." I called out in a mocking tone.

The bodyguard turned his head and looked at me. When recognition sunk in, his eyes got as big and as round as saucers. Before he had a chance to turn his gun on me, I sent two bullets to his stomach. He dropped his gun and his hands went immediately to his gunshot wound. More shots rang out. I dove into Meech and we both fell by the car.

"C'mon man!" I yelled in his face then smacked the shit out of him. He looked at me crazy but hopped up as shots continued to ring out. Whoever was trying to take him out were amateurs. Their bullets weren't even coming close to us as we ducked in between cars until we made it to my ride.

I unlocked the door and hopped in, Meech followed suit. I could hear sirens in the distance and I'd never been more happy to know the law was coming than I was at that moment. I backed out of the parking spot that I was in and hauled ass.

I headed to one of Meech's trap houses so we could lay low until shit blew over. When we pulled up, I blew the horn until a few of his goons came out of the house.

"Where the fuck y'all guns at?!" I snapped as I stepped out of the car.
Everybody looked at each other instead of answering my question.

"That's the quickest way to end up dead! If a mufucker in yo territory doing what I just did, you come out with ya guns drawn!" I snapped at them. It felt like I was schooling a bunch of young niggas when I think we're all the same damn age. "Get Meech out the car." I said as I walked past them and headed into the house. When I walked in, I couldn't believe my eyes. They had three bad ass bitches in here snorting powder with the music blasting.

"What happened to Meech?" One of the guys asked as they helped him inside. I ignored him as I walked up to the radio and turned it off.

"Heyyy!" One of the girls said in a sing song voice. "Why you turn it offff? That was my jammmm." She whined.

I frowned my face up in disgust as I looked at her.

"Have you paid yet?" I asked as I looked down on her menacingly.

Her eyes shot over in the direction of the guy that asked me what happened. I knew off top that they had been letting these hoes use the product for free. How can you possibly take over the streets when ya crew giving away product? I walked up to her and started to pat her down. She pushed my arm away and I pulled out the pistol I got from Meech. All three of them started to scream.

"Shut the fuck up!" I snapped. "Take all the dope and money out ya pockets right now."

The girl farthest away from me looked at the girl with the whiny voice.

"Bitch I knew you would get us caught!" She snapped as she started emptying her pockets.

"Fuck you Brittany!" The chick with the whiny voice said.

"No fuck you Tanya!" Brittany fired back.
They all stood up and emptied their pockets.
"You happy?" Tanya asked.
"Bitch don't try me." I stated calmly.
I pulled her shirt and unsnapped her bra. A knot of
money fell on the floor in front of her feet. I shook
my head as I nodded towards the other two. They
both raised their shirts slowly and unsnapped their
bras. Dope hit the floor. I searched everywhere but
in their pussy and put all the drugs and money on
the table.
"If I catch y'all here again." I paused as I
looked each one of them in the eye. "I will kill
you." I continued. I stood there and watched them
closely as the ran out of the door.
"Yo you bleeding." One of the goons said. I
looked at him and he was pointing at me. I quickly
gave myself a once over and saw the blood dripping
on the floor from my pants leg.
"Ah hell." I said as I took a seat on the
couch. I rolled my pants leg up and sighed with
relief. It was only a flesh wound. I got grazed. It
was nothing that couldn't heal on its own. "What's
y'all name? You start." I said as I pointed at the guy
that was standing the closest to me. I figure if I'm
going to help Meech bring order to his team, I need
to know who they are.
"Peanut."
"Skeme."
"Smoke."
"Trip." They all said one at a time.
I nodded my head as I tried to figure out who was
running this particular trap house without asking. I
couldn't tell. Neither of them looked like the boss.

"Who's in charge?" I asked and watched as they looked at each other. "Wow." I said to myself. "Aye how you know they were stealing?" Skeme asked with a serious look on his face. "If you give a bitch an inch she gone take a mile every time." I responded. Shit I thought everybody knew the basics of this shit. These niggas were just playing around. They were gone fuck around and get killed playing.

I gave them a quick run through of what happened. Neither one of them knew who it could have been that was after Meech. That meant I was about to spend all night teaching these niggas what they should and should not be doing. We had to get ready for war.

Michelle

My eyes grew big as my body was filled with awe as we pulled up to the biggest estate I had ever been to in my life. We drove through these large, black, steel gates and up a long driveway. The driveway had lights leading all the way up to the door on both sides. I can imagine it would look like a landing strip at night time.

"What's your name?" I asked once I realized I hadn't asked her anything about herself other than the question about her being a police officer.

"I'm Medusa and that is Silk." she answered just as the car came to a stop. Silk got out of the car and when I reached for the door handle, Medusa popped my other hand. I snatched it away from her and gave her a weird look. "Silk opens the doors." She said with a straight face. I nodded my head slowly. Hell if Silk wanted to go around opening everybody's doors then I guess I wouldn't be touching any.

Silk opened her door first, then came back around and opened mines. I walked around, stood behind Medusa and waited for her to lead the way. She kept her feet planted until Silk walked in front of her and lead us to the tallest doors I had ever seen in my life. There were no doorknobs on the doors at all. I frowned slightly until Silk placed both of his hands on the door and they opened. It was by far the weirdest thing I had saw so far. When we walked in, Silk and Medusa both removed their shoes so I followed suit.

"You may only go where there is black carpet. Anywhere there is white carpet is off limits." Medusa explained then walked off. "Oh yeah." She said as she stopped in her tracks. I waited for her to turn around but she never did. "Get cleaned up. Dinner is at 6:30 and your date is at 8pm." She continued.

My face crinkled up in confusion.

"My date?" I asked because she had no idea I was going to come. Hell I had no idea I was going to come. How the fuck did I end up with a date any damn way?

"Yes. That's how you will earn your stay." She said and walked off like a boss.

I hope this bitch doesn't think I'm selling pussy. She can kick rocks bare foot! Hell I'll kick rocks bare foot before I sell some pussy. *"Bitch got me fucked up!"* I thought to myself.

I followed the black carpet to the living room but nobody was in there. I began to wonder if Medusa and Silk lived here alone in this big ass house. I left out of the living room and followed the carpet to an entertainment room. There was a pool table, computer, and Pacman station inside. There were also four girls there. I walked in slowly and took a seat. They all turned around and looked at me then continued what they were doing.

I sat down and watched the quietest pool game I had ever saw in my life. Nobody talked shit or nothing as they played. I was beyond confused but more than anything, I was ready to go. I walked out of the entertainment room and down the hall. I read each name on the door as I passed them.

"Silk. Medusa. Trina. Stephanie. Megan. Ashley." I read as I continued walking. "Missy?" I said out loud to myself. My jaw hit the floor.

"I see you found your room." Medusa said. I jumped around with my hand gripping my chest tightly. She appeared, seemingly out of nowhere and scared the entire fuck out of me.

"How did you? When did you?" I asked confused. I didn't know what to ask or how to ask it. She chuckled softly to herself and flipped her long dreads over her shoulder.

"Make yourself at home, but don't forget to get cleaned up for dinner. You have a bathroom in your room." She explained then walked away.

I watched her walk away until I could no longer see her. I turned around slowly and walked in my room. Man I was having jaw dropping experiences all over this damn house. My room was immaculate! Made special. Fit for a queen.

The bed was huge! I ran around the room just because I had room to do so. I opened the bathroom door and almost screamed because it was so big! I had no idea what I needed two showers for but I would put them both to use! I ran out of the bathroom and into the closet which was stocked with clothing. I looked through the clothes and everything still had tags on it.

"Shit they're my size!" I screamed.

"Watch your language! Keep it down!" I heard Medusa say.

I jumped around startled but I didn't see her. I was beyond confused as I looked around the room. I stepped out of the closet and looked everywhere for her. I heard a chuckle and I stood still then turned around. That's when I saw an intercom on the wall.

"You were looking for me huh?" She said followed by another chuckle. I frowned my face up like she could see me. "It happens every time. Get a bath and come to dinner." She said and just like that, the room was quiet again.

I stood there for several seconds. I was stuck. I had no idea what I had gotten myself into but I was sure I would find out soon.

I took a shower and headed out of the room to have dinner. When I walked into the living room, all the girls, including Medusa, stood behind a chair. Medusa gestured towards an open chair, so I walked around the table and stood behind it. I didn't know what was going on but I was just going to follow suit. A few minutes later, Silk came into the dining room. He started on the other side of the table and greeted each girl before he pulled out their chair and allowed them to sit down.

Trina is short and brown skinned with short curly hair. She's thick in all the right places with a small stomach. Stephanie is taller than I am, caramel complexioned, skinny with super long hair. Megan is dark skinned with a big ole bubble butt. She had her hair cut in a taper fade like a guy. Then there was Ashely, short white girl with long blonde curly hair. By the time Silk got to me, the maids were bringing out our food. I nodded my head once my steak and potatoes were placed in front of me. Silk said grace and we dug in. Nobody said a word to each other as we ate.

After dinner, I followed the girls into the living room. We were all dressed and ready to go to a place we had no knowledge of. They all looked calm, so I wasn't afraid of what would happen. A different guy came to pick up each girl and my guy came last.

"Hey there beautiful. I'm Ronald." He said as he extended his hand to shake mines.

I reached my hand out and he snatched me to him. Ronald was about my height, fat, crooked teeth and bad breath. I held my breath until he released his grip. When he leaned forward and kissed the back of my hand, I wanted to go into the kitchen and cut it off.

"Let's go." He said as he practically dragged me out of the house.

We rode for about an hour before we ended up at what looked like a coliseum. We went in through the back door. I was so confused.

"Your small so they will underestimate you." He said as he shoved me into a small room. "Get dressed you have five minutes." He said then closed the door. My jaw dropped again as I turned around and looked at what I was supposed to change into.

<u>Amere</u>

I woke up to the smell of bacon. I climbed out of bed, brushed my teeth, pissed and washed my hands. I made my way to the kitchen and the sight before me made my mouth water. She stood with her back to me wearing spandex shorts and a tank top shirt that stopped about midway. I stared at her so hard that I could see her lower back muscles flex as she reached over the stove. I allowed my eyes to roam all over her body but they lingered at her thick thighs. She didn't have the biggest ass in the world but it was just right for her small frame.

"You ready to eat?" She asked. I jumped slightly but she hadn't turned around.

"Huh?" I asked. I felt like I was stuck on stupid. I shook my head at myself.

"I said are you ready to eat?" She repeated her question as she turned around slowly. She had a skillet with eggs in it, in her hand. I watched her scoop the eggs on a plate that was on the counter. That's when I realized she had a big breakfast laid out for us.

"Damn how I miss all this?" I asked myself.

"Because you were focused on all this." She said with a smile.

My mouth hung open because I hadn't realized I said that out loud.

"Close ya mouth Amere." She said as she reached over the counter. Her smile was contagious.

"What's your name?" I asked as I stared at her intensely. She shied away from my gaze as she began to pile food on a plate.

"Simone." She answered and handed me my plate of food.

She cooked pancakes, sausage, bacon, grits, eggs and hash browns. This plate made me think of Tamia. I hadn't told her I was in town yet.

"Milk or orange juice." Simone asked as I made my way out of the kitchen.

"Orange juice." I tossed over my shoulder as I made my way to my room.

I grabbed my phone and sent Tamia a text then called Meech. His ass still didn't answer. I shook my head as I made my way back into the kitchen. I sat down and ate breakfast with a total stranger as if we've known each other for a while.

"Man that was bussin but aye you heard from Meech?" I asked as I followed her into the living room. She shook her head and took a seat.

"Naw I hardly ever do. All he did was ask could you stay here 'til you got ya own shit." She replied.

I shook my head as I thought about it. That was by far the dumbest shit I had ever heard a female say.

"This nigga asked you could a stranger stay with you and you said yes?" I asked because it didn't make sense.

"Meech will never put me in harm's way. If he trusts you enough for us to meet, then I'm safe in your hands. I don't meet anybody." She answered with a straight face.

I completely understand what she's saying but that doesn't make it any less dumb. She trusts that nigga too much. I haven't even talked to Meech's ass in years so why would he trust me enough to send me to one of his people. Not that I'm going to do anything to her but shit, he ain't know that.

"So what y'all doing?" I asked just to make conversation. Naw I'm lying, if I can't get Tamia's ass back then she's the next best thing.

"He's my brother. Found out about 5 years ago." She said as she nodded her head.

That gave me the green light but I wasn't going to try to step to her. Shit if anything, I was going to have her trying to step to me.

"Ok while I'm here, I know I'm irresistible and shit, but stay in ya own room. Don't be trying sneak in my shit." I said with a serious expression although I was playing.

She laughed the sexiest laugh I had heard in a long time. I wanted to bend her little thick ass over, but I knew exactly how to get a female like her.

I think all females want to be wanted, that's why y'all be choosing assholes. The typical asshole doesn't want you and you just want him to want you. Here's a secret though, that nigga want you, he just knows you don't want a thirsty nigga.

"Thanks for breakfast." I said as I stood to my feet.

"You don't want to watch a movie or something?" She asked. I looked at her and smiled.

"I'll get up with you later." I said then went to my room and got dressed.

It was time I got out and found my cuzzo so we could link up.

Armani

Let me take a moment and be completely honest real quick. Ok, so I've always been heavier than Tamia. Shit my mouth has always been on 10. I use to snap on every fucking body, meanwhile Tamia would walk away. As long as I've known her, she has gotten in maybe four fights, give or take. Hell, she should have been fighting Lisa's ass for all of that disrespectful shit she would post about her when we all lived on the coast. Noo, not Tamia. Tamia ignored everything that bitch said to her like it was nothing. We moved to Detroit and here come Lisa and Tamia still did nothing. I thought that maybe if Lisa approached her she would flip out and she still did nothing!

That day at the mall when they ran into each other, yeah you remember the day; I talked Tamia into coming to the mall with me and we pulled up at damn near the same time as Lisa and Amere. Well um, I knew they were going. Shit to be completely honest, I wanted Tamia to whoop her ass because I was mad that I was playing second to Lisa's nothing ass! See Lisa use to post her every move on Facebook like a lot of y'all do. If I wanted to know what was up with Amere, I'd just look at Lisa's page. So yeah, I played dumb when we saw them but I already knew they were going to be there.

Now fast forward back to now! When I swung at Tamia and missed, I didn't think she was going to do a bitch ass thing, but that little mufucker gave me a run for my money. Now I'm taking my well whooped ass in here to check on my son. I shook my head as I entered his room. He was having a fit like he knew what was going on.

"What's the matter big boy?" I cooed as I picked him up. As soon as I brought him up to my chest, I knew exactly what was wrong.

"Somebody's funky wunky!" I said as I frowned my face up.

I laid him on his changing table and cleaned him up. He'd been sleep long enough to want a bottle now so I went ahead and fixed him one.

I sat in the living room and began to feed him when Tamia came from the back of the house. I looked up at her and smiled as she made her way into the living room. She had cleaned herself up and placed something on her cut. She sat down on the couch and just stared off so I knew something was up.

"What's wrong T?" I asked her. It took her a minute to respond. I wasn't going to push the issue or nothing like that because when someone is ready to talk, they will.

I leaned back against the couch and continued to feed Armad. We sat there for a good hour or so when Tamia's phone chimed on the coffee table. It went off twice and she didn't budge to touch it.

"What if it's Rashard?" I asked because curiosity was starting to get the best of me.

"I left him." She said without looking up. I was beyond confused by the statement. If she left him then where the hell did she and my son stay last night.

"Elaborate." I said. I could tell my use of the word shocked her by her facial expression. I've never been a dumb chick; I just never apply myself to anything. I waited on her to respond as I burped Armad.

Tamia gave me a little run through about how this nigga ain't been there and how they ain't been fucking in a few days. Now granted all of that is questionable but the fact this nigga came home smelling like he had just taken a shower, gave everything away.

"Wanna find her?" I asked because I hadn't beat a bitch up in a long time.

I need to get my "beat a bitch up" game up though. I'm not trying to be in the streets trying to fight and become the bitch that got beat up.

"Who?" Tamia asked. Her phone started ringing. She reached over and grabbed it. "Hey biiiitch!" She sang into the receiver all animated and shit. I rolled my eyes because she was just looking pitiful.

"Naw I'm not there. I'm gonna be staying at Mani's house til I find my own place." She said. At first I wasn't going to eavesdrop but shit this was news to me!

I mean she told me she left him but damn she ain't say she needed a place to stay hell! This was my type of tea right here. I got up to lay Armad down because I didn't want to miss a thing.

"Yeah, I'm going to text you her address." She said then hung the phone up. "Candy's here!" She said to me.

She had been trying to get Candy to come here for the longest but Candy and Deuce had moved somewhere else.

"How long she here for?" I asked just out of curiosity. I purposely didn't mention her living here because it was no problem.

"For good. She said the movers will be here tomorrow, so she's crashing here with us tonight." She said like that shit was ok.

My damn mouth was resting between my feet on the fucking floor. Why on earth would she invite someone to stay here when she hadn't talked to me? Hell she hadn't even asked me if she could stay here yet!

"I'm fina go to the store. Do you need anything?" Tamia asked as she stood to her feet. I just shook my head because had I opened my mouth, she would have been that bitch that I was going to beat the fuck up!

"Cool." she said then headed towards the door. "What the fuck?" I heard Tamia say a few seconds later.

"Where's my husband?" I heard someone ask.

"This bitch had to have had the wrong door because nobody's husband was here." I thought to myself as I walked towards the front door.

"Um ma'am. Who the hell is your husband?" I heard Tamia ask.

"Dave bitch don't play stupid!" Dave's wife snapped.

I stopped in my tracks as I gathered my thoughts. I couldn't believe this bitch came all the way to Atlanta to find her husband. Where the fuck are her children?

"The only man in here is my Godson. I suggest you leave." Tamia said in an extremely calm tone. Shit scared me a little bit. I made slow, baby steps to the door.

I know I was just talking big shit about beating a bitch up but now that I have the option, it doesn't seem like a good idea. I'm not scared or no shit like that but damn, my baby here.

"I'm not going any fucking where! Are you fucking him?!" I heard his wife ask just as I appeared. "Oh no it's you!" She said as she rushed past Tamia and came inside of my house.

I back pedaled but she was a hurt woman on a mission. "Why?!" She screamed as she grabbed me and pushed me into the wall.

I was literally stuck on stupid until she raised her hand to hit me. I kicked the bitch so hard that she flipped over my couch and hit the table. I waited for her to get up and come at me again but she didn't. I walked slowly around the couch.

"Oh my fucking gosh!" I said as my hand involuntarily flew to my mouth.

Tamia rushed to her side. When she looked up at me, she shook her head.

"She's dead." Tamia said with shock evident all over her face.

Michelle

I stared at the different colors of sports bra sets that hung before me. I decided on red and quickly changed into them. I know what you're thinking but shit the man said I have five minutes.

I'd rather do what he said and get ready for whatever than get caught blindsided. Wait, all of this shit is catching my off guard though.

"Fuck it." I said out loud to myself. I quickly changed into the panty and bra set. Then I noticed cards on the table. I walked over to them and flipped them over. I was beyond confused as I stared at them.

The top of each card had weapon of choice but instead of an actual weapon, they had pictures of bugs and animals. I stared at each card until the door opened. It startled me because I didn't know what was about to happen next.

"Let's go, you look beautiful." Ronald said as he waved me over. "No you need that." He said when I was about to sit the card down. I followed him out of the room and down a long hall. "Go in. Your opponent is already there." He said as he gave me a light shove.

I don't know what the fuck I'm supposed to do with this damn card. Nobody gave me any instructions. I was set up for failure on this one.

When I walked inside the room, there was two ladies inside. One of them was dressed like me and the other one was dressed like a referee. I hope like hell I didn't have to fight anyone because I've never been able to fight.

"Go to your corners." The ref said.

I watched the girl walk off to one corner so I went to the other one. Digital shades were placed over my eyes that covered the entire top half of my head. Everything looked like a game now. I could see my head floating in front of me. It was the weirdest thing I had ever seen. I felt someone slide what felt like sleeves, on both arms and I could see my arms on the screen. The next thing I felt was my body being wrapped. Slowly, I could see my body parts appear in front of me. It was as if I was playing a game. *"Oh yeah I can do this."* I thought to myself as I waited for further instructions.

"Run the course. Whoever put their cards in first and kills their opponent wins." I heard the ref say.

A "3" flashed across my face followed by a "2" then "GO". I took off running. I had to jump over a hurdle but I failed. When I hit my knee on it, I swear the pain felt so real. I looked next to me and the other girl had just past me. I knew I needed to beat her, so I hopped up and ran faster. When I neared her, I reached out and pushed her. I heard her scream out as she fell and rolled. I looked back and she was getting up slowly. As soon as I turned back around I had to duck. A tree branch came out of nowhere. Then out of nowhere, I was no longer on a track. I was in a house. It was pitch dark as I walked through the house slowly. I had no idea which way to go until I saw a flashing green arrow. I ran in the direction it was pointing.

"Ahhh." I yelled out as I hit the ground. The other girl close lined me. I didn't even know where she came from. I thought I left her on the track. I sat down and massaged my neck until I caught my breath.

When I stood up, I was in the desert. I looked around as I spun in circles until I spotted her running. I took off behind her but it was so fucking hot. I brushed up against a cactus as I ran past it. It burned like hell and I could feel the blood dripping.

"Aaarggh!" I screamed out as I broke a piece of the cactus and took off with it in my hand. As soon as I neared her, I threw it at her. It hit her in the back and she fell down. I ran up to her and stepped on her back as I snatched it out of her skin. We both screamed out. Right when I was about to hit her again, a slot showed up. It had a picture of a card, so I reached out and stuck the card in it. I heard the crowd cheering and that's when I saw that we were back in the room. Someone began pulling the game pieces off of me one by one until I could only see my head again. Next, the shades were removed. I looked down at my side and saw a few large scrapes.

"What the fuck?" I said out loud.

"Eat it! Eat it! Eat it!" The crowd began to chant. I didn't know what the fuck was going on. Then I noticed the other girl was sitting at a table with sushi in front of her. I walked up to her just as she picked it up and place it in her mouth. We were left in the room alone for at least thirty minutes.

I felt like a fucking caged animal the way all of those people were watching us from their seats. I realized we were both a part of some sort of game that those people probably paid big bucks to come and see. I'm just glad I won. I jumped backwards when the girl started to hold her throat. She stood up and reached out for me but dropped down to her knees. I was so confused as I watched her start to throw up. She fell over on her side and scratched at her neck. I didn't know if I was supposed to be excited but I was. She started to have a seizure and I just stood there and watched. I had no urge to help her or even yell for help. I guess one of us had to die and I'm just glad it wasn't me.

After she died, Ronald came back and got me. We stopped in some little room where they had a doctor to check my wounds. I had to get stitches but fuck that, I was alive. He led me back to the room and I put my clothes back on.

"Was she allergic to sushi?" I asked because I had no idea why that happened to her.

"You chose the pufferfish card. Pufferfish has poison in it. If it isn't prepared exactly how it should be, you will ingest the poison." He said but I was still confused.

"So she ingested the poison?" I asked because I was trying to clear shit up.

"Yes. It takes about thirty minutes to take effect but once it does, it doesn't stop until you're dead." He answered.

We pulled up to the house and Silk opened the door for me. "Good job." Silk said as he took a gold folder from Ronald and lead me in the house. I was confused and tired but my first date was a successful one.

Rashard

I could tell these niggas weren't use to not getting sleep. In this game, some days you didn't sleep and it was normal to wear the same fit two to three days in the row. Shit, when you're trapping, the grind don't stop. There's always someone lurking, waiting to catch you slipping. Meech and his crew were always slipping. Those same niggas from the club could have easily come here and bodied all of them. Luckily for them, the guys that were coming for them are amateurs.

"Man what the fuck going on?" Meech asked once he finally woke up. We all turned around and looked at him. They had laid his body on the couch last night but he fell on the floor and nobody tried to put him back.

Peanut rushed to him and gave him dap like he thought the man was dead or some shit. I can understand that they're happy that their boss is ok, but we got shit to do. Meech needs to get his ass up and get his organization together before it falls.

I gave them a few minutes to speak with Meech then I cut the shit off. "Man, y'all niggas need to boss the fuck up! Shit is about to change around here. Either you stay on board and get this money or there's the door." I said as I gestured towards the door.

This will be my first time in the spotlight because you know a nigga normally stays behind the scenes. I couldn't help but reflect on the years of being the man. Man I had a whole lot of shit going on with playing ball, going to school and running the streets. Shit wasn't as hard as you would think though. I've always been smart and cautious. I could go anywhere I wanted without a team because nobody knew who the fuck I was. This will be different because I'm going to be front and center with these niggas. I know one thing though, these mufuckers ain't fina get me killed. They ain't even close to being ready for war.

"Yo who them niggas was though?" Meech asked me like I was supposed to know. Before I could respond, his phone started to ring again. His shit had been ringing a lot. Shit I was hoping it would go dead but it didn't. "What up cuzzo?" Meech answered the phone.

I shook my head as I listened to his one sided conversation. He gave somebody the address to where we were and disconnected the call. I shook my head because I was going to need my team or what was left of it anyway. Dre's fake ass was dead and nobody had seen or heard from Twan's ass, so he may be somewhere dead too. Especially since him and Dre were click tight at all times.

I picked up my phone and called my nigga Deuce. "Finally got the stick out ya ass?" Deuce asked as he answered the phone.

I hadn't really been fucking with him since I found out his ass is married. Candy is like my sister but I knew he needed to be the one to tell her and so far he hadn't. Hell the last time I talked to Candy, she was still very much so happy and in love with his ass. They had a crib out in Louisiana.

I think we all lost touch after we left Detroit. Candy and Tamia didn't talk much anymore but that was kind of my fault. When I did that whole "coma" thing, which I admit was a bit over the top, I forced Candy not to tell Tamia. Well actually, I didn't tell her not to say shit but her loyalty to me wouldn't allow her to do something that she considered betrayal. It put her in a bad position since her and Tamia had been joined at the hip. They're both stubborn so that's why they haven't been talking. Shit Armani's triflin ass had even brought them together but after they left, it went right back to them not talking. Tamia needs a real friend in her life though and right now, I need my squad to link up. Anytime I had ever called them in the past, they came through with no questions asked. This would be different because I'm asking them to cross state lines. As much as I wanted to keep this attitude, I knew I needed to put my pride to the side.

"Shutup nigga. Aye what you got going?" I asked as I looked around the room. All eyes were on me and I knew these niggas had a lot to learn.

"Not shit man Candy left me." He said and he really didn't sound like himself at all when he said that.

"Why?" I asked because I know Candy loves that nigga. "You told her?" I asked when he didn't respond.

"Yea man." He answered somberly.

"Damn." I said as I shook my head. I needed to call and check on her because I don't want her around this bitch hurting.

"I was gone leave my wife man but it wasn't that simple." Deuce tried to explain. I hope he ain't hit Candy with that bullshit ass line.

"Why it ain't?" I asked as I walked into the kitchen. Shit was getting deep and it ain't have shit to do with these niggas that were all in my face.

"She pregnant man." Deuce answered and my jaw hit the floor.

"Your wife or Candy?" I asked once I realized I didn't know who the hell was pregnant.

"My wife man!" Deuce said with a little too much bass in his voice for my liking.

"Man how fast can you get to Atlanta?" I asked to change the subject before I snapped out.

"I'm on my way to the airport now. Candy's ass should be landing in a minute. I'm not fina lose her behind a baby that ain't mine!" Deuce said.

I had to pull the phone away from my ear. I was shocked beyond measurement to hear Deuce talk like that. I chuckled lightly as I thought about Candy's face whenever Deuce pops on her ass.

"Aye man hit my line when you land. I need you." I said to him as I waited for his response.

"Need me to round em up?" Deuce asked.

I smiled because my niggas always be right on time. My whole crew trained to go.

"Mos def!" I answered hyped up. "I'm fina send you the address. We need a lot of toys. These niggas ain't got none!" I said with a slight frown on my face. I really couldn't believe these mufuckers been making it as long as they have.

"Word? Damn." Deuce said. "But look, I'm parking at the airport. Let me hit everybody up and I'll hit you back." Deuce said to me.

"Iight bet." I said then ended the call.

When I walked back into the living room, everybody was sitting down waiting on me to tell them what to do next. I shook my head as I stood in the middle of the living room.

"So y'all check this out. I got a few of my rounds flying out here to help eliminate the threat. Meanwhile, y'all niggas gotta get ready for war." I said as I looked them all in their eyes.

Candy

My mind has been a complete mess. My life
has been a complete mess. How could the man that

I've loved all of these years, do me so bad? I inserted my headphones so Aaliyah could say the words that I wanted to say. I closed my eyes and hummed the lyrics along with her.

"How could the one I gave my heart to, break my heart so bad?
How could the one who made me happy, make me feel so sad?
Want somebody tell me? So I can understand
If you love me, how could you hurt me like that?
How could the one I gave my world to, throw my world away?
How could the one who said, "I love you" say the things you say?
How could the one I was so true to, just tell me lies?
How could the one I gave my heart to, break this heart of mine? Tell me
How could you be so cold to me, when I gave you everything?
All my love, all I had inside
How could you just walk out the door?
How could you not love me anymore?
I thought we had forever, I can't understand
How could the one I shared my dreams with, take my dreams from me?
How could the love that brought such pleasure, bring such misery?
Want somebody tell me?
Somebody tell me please!
If you love me, how could you do that to me? Tell me."

When I opened my eyes, they were filled with tears. Being hurt was beyond an understatement. Deuce and I had been together for years. I thought we would be together forever. He promised me forever, but he already had that with someone else. I found out Deuce was married, and not only is he married, but she's pregnant! I'm so glad I never took myself off birth control when he asked. I shook my head at the thought of us both possibly being pregnant at the same time! That's some Peter Gunz type shit that I want no part of. That's why as soon as he decided to be honest with me, I didn't respond. Hell, I didn't even pack a bag. I nodded my head and walked out of the door.

He followed me out the door screaming my name but nothing he could have ever done would have made me stay. See, I know my worth and I won't settle for shit. Naw, I'll leave the settling for the females that haven't established what they deserve. See I know I deserve to be happy so happy I will be. I promise after tonight, there will be no more tears shedding for that man or any man for that matter. I don't mind heart break, this ain't the first time and I'm almost certain it won't be the last time.

Maybe this was exactly what I needed. I hadn't talked to Tamia much since we moved to two different states, but I knew that she would answer. It's just the kind of friends we are. We don't have to talk every day. We are both aware that we have lives of our own. Just know that this link up is about to be real!

The cab that I was riding in pulled up to the address that Tamia told me we would be staying at. I called her phone but she didn't answer. "I guess my pity party is over." I said to myself as I pulled my headphones out of my ears. I stuck my phone down in my pocket, paid the cabbie and walked inside of the building. I had to go up to the third level to get to the condo rise that I was looking for. These things really aren't even made like actual condos so I think that's just the name of them.

Right when I was about to knock on the door, the finest specimen of a man I'd seen in a long time stepped out of another condo. He was tall as fuck and about as chocolate as he was tall. He had a fresh fade with waves so deep I wanted to get naked and take a swim. My eyes roamed down to his chest and arms. *"Oh gosh those muscles."* I thought to myself as my mouth watered. I couldn't believe my body responded to this man the way it was but I like it!

"How are you?" He asked me.
I stared at him with probably the dumbest look on my face he had ever seen. I can only imagine how I looked with my mouth open. He took a step closer and his cologne engulfed my nostrils. I closed my eyes as I inhaled deeply. When I opened my eyes back, he was smiling. He had perfect teeth! I've always been a sucker for teeth!

"What's your name?" I asked him.
"James. James Steele." He answered as he extended his hand in my direction.
I placed my small hand in the palm of his large hand. I watched slowly as he brought my hand up to his lips. I had to look down to make sure there wasn't a puddle on the floor between my legs because his soft kiss did something to me.

"Do I have to ask your name Miss Lady?" He asked with that beautiful smile again.

"I'm sorry. Um, my name is Candy." I said to him. I noticed we were still holding hands but I didn't mind at all. I could definitely get busy with that fine specimen of a man.

"Well I have to get going. Maybe I'll catch you later." He said then kissed my hand again before he let it go.

I watched that man walk down the hall. Hell I watched him until he got on the elevator. Shit I was still looking after the elevator doors closed! "Damn." I whispered under my breath. I turned around and knocked on the door. It took a minute but Tamia swung the door open.

"Damn bitch what happened to you?" I asked referring to the knot on her head that had a damn Band-Aid on it.

They should have gotten Doc's ass to move up here with them. Tamia didn't respond, she snatched me in the apartment.

"What the fuck?" I asked with my face frowned up. I felt like I was on an emotional rollercoaster the way mufuckers was causing my moods to hop around.

"Bitch listen." Tamia said but the way Armani was pacing back and forth had my attention on lock. "Candy!" Tamia said as I continued to look at Armani. I didn't know what the fuck they had going on. Shit if Tamia wasn't in here, I'd walk right back out the door and I haven't even found out what happened yet. Tamia grabbed my face to make me look at her. I frowned and shoved her back softly. Just enough to let her know not to grab my damn face.

"Armani's dude-"

"He's not my fucking dude!" Armani yelled cutting Tamia off. Tamia rolled her eyes and continued.

"His wife came in here and attacked Armani." Tamia said then closed her eyes.

"Ok and? What y'all do, kill the bitch?" I asked with a laugh. I didn't stop laughing until I noticed neither of them joined in on the laughter. "Tamia!" I said as I looked at her with a shocked expression on my face. "You killed her?" I asked and she didn't respond.

I knew by her not responding that it wasn't her. I was not about to let her go down for some shit she ain't have shit to do with. Armani's hoe ass should leave people men alone and maybe their wives won't show up. But then again, who am I to talk? I'd been with a nigga for years that turned out to be someone else's husband.

I walked further into the house and saw the bitch sprawled out on the living room floor. I could see clearly that she hit her head on something and bled out. I grabbed my phone and called the only person that I knew would come through.

"I'm a little busy right now." He said as he answered the phone. If he was that damn busy he wouldn't have answered.

"I need you boss." I said with panic in voice.

"What's wrong?" He asked. I could tell he was worried.

"Can't say. Come to Armani's house right now." I said then hung the phone up.

I had no idea what to do but I knew he would. Plus, Tamia is here and if that nigga will do anything for anybody, it's her.

I know he doesn't really act like he gives a fuck about her but I think his ass would be sick if she didn't come back home to him after this shit. I don't think he even knows she's leaving him.

"Who was that?" Armani asked. I tried to ignore the daggers that Tamia kept throwing at me with her eyes but she started sighing heavily.

"Why did you call him?" Tamia asked.

"Ooooh!" Armani said then laughed.

"Because he will know what to do so nobody goes to jail!" I snapped because she was being extra fucking petty right now.

"It was self-defense!" Tamia screamed.

"And where do you work Armani? Is this in your name? If so, where are your check stubs? Why was she here? Was her man just here? Are you still sleeping with him?" I fired off question after question.

I could see the anger rising within Armani but I had a point to prove.

"Do you want them asking you all of those questions? I guarantee you the police will find a way to flip it on you. Even if they don't, they still gone arrest you until they figure it out." I said then shrugged my shoulders.

I had never seen Armani cry before that very moment but she broke down. Tamia and I looked at each and shrugged our shoulders.

Michelle

"How'd it go?" Medusa asked once I stepped out of the shower in my room. I was completely naked and she didn't give a fuck. She stood in the bathroom with me like I was fully dressed.

"I won." I said as I began to dry my body off with the towel.

"I know that much but how do you feel about it?" She asked as she continued to stare at me. I shifted my body slightly because it felt like she could see inside of my soul. *"You need to get the fuck outta there."* I heard Missy say in my head. I didn't respond because she wasn't saying shit I wasn't already thinking.

"It's not something I want to do again." I said as I looked away from her.

I probably should have kept my eyes on her and I would have saw her coming before I felt her. My body was lifted in the air and tossed into the mirror. It shattered upon impact but none of the pieces fell.

"You will do as you are told!" Medusa snapped as she looked at me.

"Kill her!" Missy screamed but I shook my head.

"No? You saying no to me?" Medusa asked.

She confused my shake of the head for responding to her and not Missy. I sighed heavily as I looked at Medusa with a horror filled face. I wasn't the least bit afraid of her but sometimes you have to play the fool long enough to fool the fool. I didn't mind killing mufuckers until I had a chance to leave. They won't be able to keep me here long.

"Get dressed you have a date." Medusa said and I frowned at her in confusion.

"I just had a date." I said to her. She turned around so fast that one of her dreads slapped me in the mouth.

"And?" She asked. I just shook my head.

"You should kill her!" Missy said.

I knew if all else failed that Missy would get us out of here. They have no idea who they're dealing with.

I climbed off the sink slowly and grabbed another outfit out of the closet. I got dressed and made my way to the front of the house. Trina, Stephanie and Megan were all sitting in the living room watching TV as quiet as church mice.

"Where's Ashley?" I thought to myself.

"This way." Silk said as he opened the front door for me.

I stole one last glance into the living room. Ashley was looking at me with a sad expression on her face. I felt Silk tug at my arm to get me to keep it moving. I followed him outside to one of those long Lincoln Town cars. Silk opened the door for me and I slid in the back seat.

"You have two hours." Silk said then closed the door.

"How are you?" The guy in the back seat asked.

When I glanced over at him I had to do a double take. First of all, he smelled good as fuck! Second of all, he looked good as fuck! I know I said I wouldn't sell no pussy for them but shit! I might have to take that back.

"I'm sore. How are you?" I asked and his smile went away.

"Don't ask me questions." He said with a straight face.

"Oh... Kay." I said as I faced the front of the car. I kept my hands intertwined between my legs until we pulled up at the Ritz Carlton.

"Are you hungry my love?" He asked with a smile that showcased the most beautiful teeth I'd ever seen. I couldn't help but smile back although I thought he was crazier than I am.

"A little." I replied hesitantly. I didn't really know what to say because I didn't know what would set him off. The driver got out and opened his door for him. I waited patiently, as still as possible because I was told not to touch a door.

I was slick scared that had I reached to open the door he would go crazy. The driver came around on my side and opened my door so I stepped out. My date extended his hand out for mine so I gave it to him. We walked hand in hand to the restaurant that I found out they had just opened inside of the hotel. Apparently, it was something new they were trying out.

I'm going to call my date Buddy since I don't know his name and I'm scared to ask him anything about himself. So, Buddy ordered our food then lead me to the room I think we will be staying in tonight.

When I opened my plate, he had ordered me shrimp and lobster. I waited for him to give me the ok that I could eat the food without him flipping out on me.

After I was done eating, I sat still so I could figure out what we were going to do.

"Let's play a game!" He said and I could tell he was excited. My first thoughts went to the game I played where I could feel everything that was happening.

"As long as it doesn't hurt." Is what I wanted to say. "Sure." is what rolled off my tongue effortlessly.

"Ok, so I have these cards that will tell us what to do to the other one. We have to play naked though." He explained.

I was a bit skeptical but I stood up and undressed anyway. He crawled on the bed then helped me on the bed. He laid the cards on the bed face down so we couldn't see what they said. He grabbed some dice off the table and handed them to me. I took a deep breath and rolled the die. "7." Then he rolled. "9." *"Ah fuck I lost."* I thought to myself as he smiled mischievously. He grabbed a card, read it then sat it on the night stand. He got on his knees and I couldn't help but admire his toned, muscular frame. He pushed me over gently, so I laid all the way back. He grabbed my titty and sucked my nipple into his mouth. He twirled his tongue around it then sucked it back in. I tried to fight the urge to moan but I lost. I could feel my pussy getting wet, then he stopped.

I sighed heavily as I sat back up. I stared at him as he sat back down and waited on me to pull a card.

"Nibble on their ear for fifteen seconds." Is what the card said.

I got up on my knees and reached over to him. I pushed him over and took his soft dick in my mouth. I sucked it until it got hard again. I continued to suck and slobber all over it. I stroked the shaft as I sucked. Buddy moaned out.

"Ouch!" I said as my body flew off the bed. When I looked up at him, I was slightly dizzy. He had punched me in the side of the head. I sat on the floor and rubbed my face as I cried.

"Get dressed!" He snapped. "I guess I wasn't moving fast enough because he jumped off the bed and snatched me to my feet. "That card didn't say that!" He snapped as he pushed me roughly towards the table.

I got dressed and he lead me back to the car. When we pulled back up to the house I didn't know what to do. Silk opened the door and helped me out.

"Why are you back so soon?' Silk asked Buddy.

"She didn't follow directions." I heard Buddy say then the car pulled off. I was so scared that I didn't even look at Silk.

"I thought you would do well." Silk said with a voice filled with disappointment. "Go to your room." He demanded as he pulled Medusa to the side. I felt like a kid about to get a whooping as I waited for my punishment.

"This can't be life." I said as I sat down on the bed.

Rashard

I was a bit tied up with trying to get these niggas ready for war when Candy called but she all but sent me a distress signal. There was no way I was going to leave her hanging. Especially not when she was sounding the way she was sounding.

"Aye I'mma get up with you niggas in a hot second." I said as I dapped them up. I left Meech's gun on the table in case some shit popped off. I hope like hell he knows how to aim and squeeze. Well shit I hope he remembers how. I don't understand how we were on the block together and now this nigga in the A acting like he's brand new. He's going to fuck around and get himself and his team killed on the dumb shit.

I left out of the house, hopped in my car and drove to Armani's crib. I have no idea why she's there any fucking way. She probably rode with Tamia over there or something. Just as I was pulling off the street, my phone started to ring.

"Yeah?" I answered without looking at the screen. "I've been texting you." She whined in my ear. I sighed heavily as I waited for my turn to pull off into traffic.

"What's up Natasia?" I asked.

"I cooked for you last night and you didn't come back. I even cooked for you this morning." She said and I frowned my face up. The way I left, she should have known I wasn't coming back then.

"I'm grinding. It's gone be a minute." I said to her. Natasia was always cooking for a nigga but I've never had any of her food. Either I'm not hungry or just don't come back but she still cooks for me.

Now there was this one time that I was about to eat but my mom called me and I got distracted talking to her and my nieces and nephew. I missed them so much and after all of this was over, I was going to fly them out for a few days.

"Well I'm waiting. I love you." She said and I hung the phone up.

That's another thing, she says she loves me a lot. Then there's Tamia, the one I actually love and her ass never says it to me. I know our shit been rocky since the beginning but damn, niggas want to know how you feel too.

I turned the radio up as I cruised to Armani's house. I needed to hurry up and handle this shit with Candy so I could get back to what I was doing. I hadn't decided yet if Natasia needed us to have another talk or not but if she did, it would have to wait.

I pulled up to Armani's place, grabbed my pistol and stuck it down in my waistband. I rode the elevator up and knocked on the door. Candy opened the door which was weird to me, because this is Armani's crib and she and Armani aren't even like that for her to be answering her door and shit. I shrugged it off and walked inside of the condo. The first person I noticed was Tamia. She was sitting on a barstool with a knot on her head and a mean mug on her face. I knew she was mad at me but I didn't know how she got hurt. I walked straight up to her and stood between her legs. She refused to look at me.

"Baby what happened to you?" I asked with concern evident in my voice. I reached out to caress her face but she slapped my hand away. "I'm sorry baby. I shouldn't have said those things to you."

I apologized because I already knew what her problem was. I should have apologized last night but I didn't think she cared. I stared at her and waited for her to respond but she didn't.

"There's more pressing issues at this moment." Candy said.

I looked over at her and she pointed into the living room. When I turned around, there was some bitch dead on the floor by the couch.

"She did that to you?" I turned around and asked Tamia but she didn't respond. I just wanted her to say something to me but she wouldn't. My words shouldn't have been enough for her to act like this.

"We need you to get rid of her." Candy said. I sighed and turned back around. I shook my head.

"Who is she?" I asked Candy and she shrugged her shoulders.

"Dave's wife. She came here looking for him and attacked me. I kicked her, she died." Armani said as she came down the hall holding Armad.

I nodded my head and took him from her arms. He smiled up at me as I made faces at him. I walked up to Tamia with him.

"You ready for this?" I asked her with a smile on my face. I only grabbed him because I know he's a soft spot for Tamia but she didn't say anything.

"I should have knocked her ass up." I thought to myself. If I get her pregnant she will be stuck with me forever. I know that's a fucked up way to think but shit, she will have to talk to me rather she wants to or not for the sake of the kid. I smiled at the thought and sat Armad in her lap. She cradled him in her arms for a few seconds then climbed off the barstool and left. I shook my head because that girl is too damn stubborn.

"Ok where she from? How she get here?" I turned around and asked. Candy shrugged her shoulders so I looked towards Armani to answer.

"She lives in Detroit. She drove here because her husband was just here." Armani said like it was nothing.

I shook my head because I don't understand how females like that think.

"Why?" I asked because I'm curious as to why he was here. Don't get it twisted, I don't want her little slut bucket ass. I just want to know her thought process.

"Why what?" She asked as she stood to her feet with an attitude.

"Why was he here?" I asked with a straight face.

"Ok now is not the time. Can we get her out of here then worry about it?" Candy asked.

I could tell it was a touchy topic for her given her situation, but it isn't the same. Candy wasn't in the wrong and she left him when she found out. His married ass just ended up following her here though. I shook my head at the thought.

"How about we get her out of here then don't worry about Armani's pussy?" Armani snapped with a roll of her neck.

"Right especially since Armani doesn't even worry about her pussy." I said sarcastically.

"What's that supposed to mean?" She yelled. Before I could respond, there was a knock at the door. I looked at them in case they knew of someone else who was supposed to be coming.

"Get da door!" I snapped at Armani. The bitch was standing there looking stupid like this ain't her house.

I looked towards the back of the house and Tamia still hadn't resurfaced. Her little ass must be real pissed off because I didn't come home.

<u>Armani</u>

I'm so tired of mufuckers judging me. Nobody gave me any credit when I was changing but the first mistake I make; they want to call me out on it. Who the fuck is Rashard to come in here asking questions anyway? I shook my head as I made my way to the door. I made another mistake and that was opening the door without looking out the peephole.

"What are you doing here?" I asked with panic evident in my voice. I blocked his path from entering and he gave me a suspicious look. "We need to talk." He said.

I rolled my eyes and sighed dramatically.

"We talked enough! Go home and talk to your wife!" I snapped then tried to close the door. He blocked it by putting his foot in the way.

"Mani baby I'm sorry about that but listen. I came to warn you. She's on her way here." He rushed out with an apologetic expression on his face.

"Well thanks for the heads up Daddy. If she come here I'm not going to open the door. Now you should leave before she catches you here." I said to him. When what I said registered, he nodded his head and walked away.

I closed the door and locked it. *"This can't be life!"* I thought to myself as I walked back into the living room.

Her body wasn't there anymore and there was blood on my carpet. "Bitch fucked my damn carpet up!" I said out loud to myself. Candy gasped and when I looked at her, she actually looked shocked by what I had said.

"Where he take her?" I asked Candy. She shook her head and pointed towards the back of the house. I sighed dramatically and headed to the only place I knew he would have taken her.

"Who was at the door?" He asked without turning around. For a brief second, I wondered how he knew I was there. That thought faded away as I wondered why it matters to him who was at my damn door any fucking way.

"Don't worry about it. They're gone." I answered as I watched him cut at her fingertips. "What are you doing?" I asked out of curiosity. I knew Rashard didn't like me and trust me, after getting to know him this past year, the feeling is mutual.

He ignored me as he continued to cut away at her skin. It seems like it would be easier to just cut her whole finger off. I didn't say anything though because they say he knows more than me. So if he wants to keep wasting time scraping skin off then that's on him.

I walked to my room to check on Tamia. Since Rashard got here, she's been hiding out with Armad. When I walked in my room, she was texting on her phone. Considering her man is here along with both of her only friends, I began to wonder who she was talking to.

"Are you ok?" I asked as I walked all the way in and flopped down on the bed.

"You're the one that just killed a lady." She responded snidely.

I rolled my eyes but didn't respond. I knew she was just aggravated with Rashard and was taking it out on me. I guess I should have just stayed up front with Candy.

"You know if you need to talk I'm here right?" I asked just as her phone chimed again.

She ignored what I said as she checked her message. I glanced over and couldn't believe my eyes. How can she easily get a man to fall on bended knee for her? What the hell is she doing that I'm not? Lose one man and snag up your old one like it ain't nothing. I stood up and snatched Armad out of her hands.

"The fuck you doing?" She asked as she dropped her phone in an attempt to keep from dropping Armad. I had a firm grasp on my child. I was not about to let him fall.

"Bitches won't let me be great!" I tossed over my shoulder as I walked out of my room. I headed straight to the bathroom.

"Hey Rashard." I called out but got distracted. He stood upright with his shirt off as he waited for me to say whatever I was going to say.

My clit jumped at the sight before me. I walked out of the bathroom and laid Armad in his bed then returned to the bathroom. I walked all the way in and closed the door behind me.

"Wait a minute na." Rashard said with his hands extended to me. I turned around and locked the door then stripped down to nothing. I hopped on the sink and slid my finger down between my legs and began to play with my pussy.

Rashard stared at me with lust filled eyes as I took care of myself. I used my free hand to motion for him to come closer. He wiped his hands off on his pants then made his way to me.

I watched him look down at my pussy and lick his lips. He grabbed my legs and pulled me to the edge of the counter then squat down in front of me. He blew lightly on my clit. I moaned out in pure ecstasy and in anticipation of what was to come. He began to spread my pussy lips apart and lick slowly on both sides of my clit before taking it in his mouth. He sucked aggressively until my legs started to tremble. For the first time in my life, I was afraid of the orgasm that was coming. I tried to close my legs but he used his arms to pry them back open. He looked up at me and winked as he continued to suck the life out of me. I closed my eyes so tight as I braced myself for the nut that was about to shake the fucking planet.

"Man what the fuck you doing?!" Rashard snapped at me.

I opened my eyes and snatched my hand out of my panties. My face flushed with embarrassment when I realized none of what I had imagined had actually happened.

"I'm, I'm." I couldn't get it out. I wanted to apologize. I needed to apologize. But I was stuck. Rashard continued to give me the look of death as I backpedaled slowly out of the bathroom's doorway.

My son started to wiggle in my arms and that's when I realized, I had never taken him in his room to begin with. I couldn't believe myself. I had done so well these last 6 months not having sex at all. Then Dave come through and I revert right back to the Armani I use to be.

I heard someone suck their teeth and when I looked up, it was Candy. I sighed because I was just happy that it wasn't Tamia. I ran to Armad's room, laid him down then ran out the door.

"Armani where you going like that?" Candy asked. I didn't respond as I ran past the elevator and to the stairwell entrance.

It wasn't until I made it in the lobby that I realized why Candy asked where I was going like that. I thought she meant with an attitude but she meant with what I had on. I quickly closed my robe as the people in the lobby gawked at me with their noses turned up.

"Wait a minute. Is that?"

My breath got caught in my throat as he turned around slowly. I took slow jagged breaths as I backpedaled towards the door I had just run out of. This can't be life right now. I tried to make a clean getaway back up the stairs without being seen. It was like everyone grew quiet except for slight whispers. Some people pointed at me while others pulled their phones out. I knew all of this was going on but I couldn't tear my eyes away from him.

I backed up as slow as possible but when I opened the door, it made a loud squeaky noise. That's when our eyes connected. I froze in place as if being still was enough to hide me. He smiled brightly so I knew he knew exactly who I was although we had only encountered each other once.

All of a sudden, my flight or fight senses kicked in and I high tailed it back up the stairs. If he was looking for us, he obviously didn't know exactly where we were or he wouldn't have been in the lobby.

I ran non-stop until I got back to my house. I burst in, slammed the door and locked it. It wasn't until I felt safe again that I began to catch my breath. We can't go through this again. It's been a year of no drama for Christ's sake so why now?

"What's wrong?" Candy asked as she looked at me with a confused look on her face. I just stared at her. None of this would have happened if the people from our past would have just stayed where they were.

"Tamia!" Candy screamed.

I jumped up and dove for her to cover her mouth. She stepped out of the way and pushed me down on the floor.

"The fuck is your problem?!" She screamed at me.

"Ssssh!" I begged her to be quiet.

"What the fuck going on?" Tamia asked. A knock on the door stopped me from answering her question.

Michelle

Medusa beat me for hours on end like I was a fucking child. I begged Missy to help but she never came to my rescue. For the first time in my life, she wasn't there for me. Missy had always protected me and I've always taken her for granted. It may be time for me to let her take over or learn how to protect myself.

As Silk stared down at my bruised body in disgust from the door, I began to wonder what would Missy do? Had Medusa come in here with a belt and hit Missy, what would she have done?

"Go take a bath." Silk demanded as he shook his head at me.

I just laid on the ground and stared at him. I know this nigga know I can't fucking move. Why won't they just go on about their business?

"Go. Take. A. Bath. NOW!" Silk demanded. I didn't care how loud he screamed at me, it won't take the pain away. If anything, it's going to give me a headache. I rolled my eyes and sighed heavily. I allowed my body to lay completely back on the floor.

I heard Silk's footsteps coming towards me at a rapid pace but I didn't budge. He snatched me up from the floor aggressively. Again, I wished Missy would take over but she didn't. I couldn't help but think this is all karma from all the pain I'd caused and helped cause in people's lives. Between

Missy and I, I'll probably be reaping what we've sowed until I die.

Silk carried me into the bathroom by my arm. I didn't kick, scream or fight as I dangled in the air. He tossed me into the empty tub. I groaned out in pain as my body collided with the porcelain tub. I watched Silk through teary eyes as he placed the stopper in the tub and turned on the hot water. It was so hot that my nose started to sweat from the heat as the water filled the tub and soothed my aching body.

He turned around, grabbed bath beads and sprinkled them in the water. I was beyond confused but I knew this was a kind gesture. In his own way, he thought he was helping me. For that, when I kill him, I'll make it quick.

I closed my eyes and relaxed in the tub. That hot water felt so good that I stayed in it until it turned cold. I bathed slowly in the cold water then climbed out of the tub. My body ached something serious but I knew I couldn't stay here. I walked out of the bathroom and got dressed in the clothes that I had on when I first arrived here.

I laid down in the bed and listened for any noises but didn't hear anything. That wasn't unusual though because everyone is oddly quiet all the time. I don't know how Medusa trained those other girls to do that but I'll never be able to be quiet all the time. I never even hear them talk to each other. I stayed in bed for about two hours then I crept out of my room. I didn't bother to peak in anyone's room because I know they're all in bed already. I'm just trying to get myself out of here, fuck them other bitches.

I made sure I stayed on the black carpet until I made my way into the kitchen. I found two knives and used my shoestrings to tie them to my ankle in case I needed to defend myself. I walked out of the kitchen and up to the front door. Disappointment set in quickly once I realized that nobody can open these doors but Silk. Is it not Medusa that's the boss? I reflected on every time a door opens, it's because Silk opened it.

"What the fuck is going on here?" I asked myself out loud as I stared at the door.

"You tell me." Silk said from behind me. I whipped around and stared at him but didn't respond.

"What are you doing?" Silk asked with an unreadable expression on his face.

"I just want to leave. I don't want any problems." I said with my hands up.

His facial features softened as he nodded his head.

He walked towards me but I didn't budge. He stopped directly in front of me and clenched his jaws. I'd been through so much in life that it would take a lot more than a little jaw flexing to scare me.

"You want to leave and go where?" He asked. At this point we were so close that I could feel his breath tickle my forehead as he waited for me to answer his question.

"Anywhere but here." I replied honestly.

All I wanted to do was get the hell away from him and Medusa and these weird ass dates! I did not have time to be getting beat the fuck up for nothing. Hell I'm the one that had a mission that I'm just about ready to get back on.

I'd been so focused on staying off the radar that I completely lost sight of why I was staying under the radar in the first place. If it wasn't for Tamia and Rashard, I'd still have my man and sweet job at Carte Blanche. Now I bet they're somewhere living it up, probably married with kids by now. Meanwhile, I been underground and now that I've resurfaced, I'm still doing underground type of shit. I don't know where these crazy fucks came from but it's a whole lot of them around here. I need to leave here and catch a bus to Detroit so I can finish what we started.

"Ok." Silk said and I gave him a confused look.

"I can go?" I asked. I couldn't help but think that this is some type of joke. Why would they keep me in a place with no fucking door knobs, beat me and force me on weird ass dates then just let me go?

"Yes. It's against the law to hold anyone against their will. Remember, you came willingly. Those dates, nobody forced you." He said to me. I couldn't help but think that everything he was spitting was bullshit and as soon as I left, he would kill me.

"Are you going to kill me?" I asked seriously. He shook his head no then walked past me. I watched him walk up to the door and place his hands firmly against it.

For the first time I heard a click, then they opened slowly. He gestured for me to leave with a simple head nod. I looked at him suspiciously as I past him and walked onto the porch.

"Y'all not going to come looking for me?" I asked just to be sure. He shook his head. "And just so we're clear. None of you are going to kill me?" I asked as I pointed towards the house.

"No." he paused then glanced behind me. "They are." He continued then slammed the door.

Tamia

I was beyond aggravated with everything that had taken place in this short amount of time. I know they say when it rains, it pours but damn! Can I please get a break? Like an actual happy break. Maybe take a vacation and get away from the everyday stresses of working forty plus hours a week while trying to start my own clinic. All I want is time to be happy with myself. I don't need Rashard to be happy because I love myself enough to go anywhere in this world alone and make it. Self-love is the best love. I've had a wall up my whole life and for good reason.

I know people have called me selfish but those people don't even know me. If focusing on school to better myself and leaving my boyfriend without a second thought after he cheated makes me selfish, then I guess I am. If going off to college and graduating with honors in order to get the degree that I knew I deserved because I worked my ass to get it makes me selfish, then I guess I am. If not letting the actions of others bother me to a point that I break down every time some shit pops off make me selfish, then I guess I am. I disagree with the fact that I'm selfish completely though. There's not a selfish bone in my body. Hell yeah I care about myself more than I care about anyone else, but so should you. I don't have children or family, so please enlighten me on who I should love more than me.

As I looked at the scene before me, I couldn't help but think that I shouldn't be here. This shouldn't be my life. Candy stood against the wall with a frown etched on her face, so I'm sure she felt the exact same way. Rashard looked like he wanted to throw up on Armani. Then when my eyes landed on her, she looked like she had seen a ghost. Her skin grew pale as whoever was at the door continued to knock. I looked between her and door as I tried to figure out if I should answer it or not. Clearly, she wasn't going to answer it.

"Who is it Mani?" I asked but she was stuck on stupid.

She just stared at me and shook her head as fresh tears stung her cheeks. I couldn't understand why she was so afraid. The only person she had ever been that afraid of was Steve and he was long gone. Dead as a door knob. I walked up to her and got on my knees in front of her.

"It's going to be ok. They can't take us all." I said in her ear as I hugged her tight around her neck. Her body went limp so I pulled back and looked at her face.

"I thought you killed him T." she said as she looked at me. "I think he's here for you." She continued. In that moment, I think my heart stopped as a huge lump got lodged in my throat.

Here I am trying to comfort her when the man at the door is here to kill me. Maybe not kill me. Well shit if I tried to kill him, then he has to be here on some revenge type of shit.

I stood to my feet and looked back at Rashard. He hadn't heard anything Armani had said and neither did Candy, so they were standing there waiting to see what would happen next. The knocking on the door continued. Again, I looked from the door to Armani. She shook her head in an attempt to warn me. I gave her a soft smile and stepped over her so I could get right up to the door.

He knocked harder just as I looked through the peephole.

"Oh my gosh." I said out loud as shock registered.

"What? Who is it?" Candy asked.

"I got this." I said to Candy as thoughts of what Brandon had done to her and Myra flashed through my head. I could not allow him to come in here and hurt anyone here because of me.

If all I have to do is surrender myself to him then I will, but he won't hurt any of the people in here. I looked at Candy and smiled because she had a confused expression on her face.

I got back on my knees so I could whisper something to Armani. Her eyes got big as they filled with tears. "Please." I begged as I looked at her. She nodded her head and hugged me tight. I stood back up and looked at Rashard who had a frown on his face. Armani stood to her feet as well. I knew she was getting ready to do what I asked her to do. I took a deep breath just as he started knocking on the door again. I thought it was strange that he never said a word as he knocked. How does he even know he has the right door? I moved towards Rashard and wrapped my arms around his neck. He hugged me tight then looked down in my eyes. I kissed him like I'd never see him again, because I probably wouldn't.

"I love you." I said to him for the first time. He frowned slightly as his eyes filled with mist. "I-" he paused and cleared his throat.

"I love you too." He said without breaking eye contact.

I stepped out of his embrace and backpedaled to the door. I nodded my head at Armani, smiled at Candy then turned around.

"What's going on?" Rashard asked just as I placed my hand on the doorknob. I didn't respond. I sighed heavily as I fought to keep my tears at bay.

I opened the door, stepped out into the hallway and closed it behind me. I heard the door lock as soon as it closed. I released a breath of relief then looked up to face him.

"Did you know I was coming for you?" Brandon asked as he grabbed my arm and pulled me towards the emergency exit stairwell.

I didn't respond to him. There was no need to. I didn't even know he was alive; so how would I have known that he'd be coming for me?

"I didn't think it would be this easy." Brandon said with a voice filled with excitement as we walked briskly through the lobby.

I could feel someone staring at me so I looked around the lobby.

"Oh you think someone's coming to save you?" Brandon asked once he noticed how I looked around the lobby.

My eyes landed on a familiar face just as he looked up at me. I thought he was dead as well.

"What the fuck is going on?" I thought to myself as I continued to stare at him with a questioning look in my eyes.

Rashard

I don't know what the fuck just happened but all I could think about was the way Tamia looked at me when she told me she loved me. Although it was her first time saying it, it felt like a final goodbye. I didn't know what to think or do as she walked out of the door but I knew something wasn't right. Armani stood guard at the door like I couldn't move her if I needed to. I just didn't know what was going on.

"What was that about?" Candy asked Armani who continued to stand at the door like a guard dog with tears streaming down her face. "Who was that?" Candy asked once she didn't respond.

She lowered her eyes to the ground then my phone started to ring. I pulled it out and glanced at the screen. It was Natasia but she would have to wait.

I stuck my phone back in my pocket as I waited for Armani to tell us who Tamia stepped outside of the door to talk to.

"Brandon." She said then Candy gasped.

I looked over at Candy who had started crying instantly at the mention of his name. My eyes shot back over to Armani as she stood in front of the door.

I walked up to the door but she continued to block my path.

"Move." I said to her as calm as I could in that moment. She shook her head no. "Listen to me carefully. I will knock yo mufucking ass out without a second thought if you don't move." I promised her.

Don't get me wrong, I don't put my hands on women but I will knock this bitch out if she don't move so I can make sure Tamia is ok.

"She don't want you to come out there." Armani croaked out. I could tell she didn't want to block the door forreal. This was her last attempt at being a friend. Another poor attempt if I may say so myself.

"What did she say to you?" Candy asked her.

I had completely forgotten that Tamia whispered something in her ear before she left.

"She told me that he only wants her but if he gets in here, he will kill us all." She said and my jaw hit the floor.

I pushed Armani out the way and snatched the door open. My heart cracked when I stepped into an empty hallway.

"Tamia!" I screamed as I ran down to the elevator.

It was taking too long so I ran to the stairwell.

"Tamia!" I screamed as I ran down the three flights of stairs. I ran out into the lobby and continued to scream her name. Everybody was looking at me like I was crazy. "Tamia!" I screamed as I looked in every face that was in the lobby.

I ran out the door in search of her and continued to scream her name but to no avail. She was gone. "Fuck!" I screamed out as I continued to search through the dark parking lot. I had no idea what Brandon was driving now. Hell, I thought his ass was dead. My phone started to ring again.

"Man what?!" I snapped without looking at the receiver.

"You lost something?" A familiar voice asked. I frowned my face up because I couldn't put a name to the voice.

"What?" I asked just to get him to talk again.

"Should I have said someone?" He asked then the line went dead.

"No! Shit! Call back!" I said out loud like they could hear me.

I checked my call log but the number was blocked. I heard sadistic laughter nearby. I looked around in attempt to find the culprit. Whoever had just called me was still here. They were watching me.

"Come out!" I yelled as I waited for them to say anything so I would know exactly where they were. There was nothing. Complete silence until the flashlight cop came towards me. I shook my head and walked past him.

"Sir." he called out but I continued to walk away. I didn't have time for this shit. I needed to get my girl back safely. I swear if that nigga hurt her I'm going to kill him and Armani.

"Sir! I'm going to call the police." He said and it stopped me in my tracks. The first thing I thought about was the dead bitch that was in Armani's tub. If the police came, they would undoubtedly end up in the apartment. I wasn't about to go to jail.

"That would be unnecessary." I said to the flashlight cop as I turned back around.

"What seems to be the problem then?" He asked. I could tell he just wanted to be nosey.

"My girl went through my phone while I was painting a canvas for our Godson." I explained.

I had no idea where that lie came from but it actually made sense. Especially since I had just noticed the blood stains on my pants leg. It was a good thing that he didn't know the difference. Well if he could, he couldn't tell.

"Damn son. I'm sure she will come around." He said then patted me on the shoulder. I nodded my head and headed back up to Armani's place.

My phone started to ring again. I sighed heavily and answered the phone.

"Baby when you coming back? I cooked for you." Natasia said in my ear.

I swear her ass is always cooking for a nigga. You would think that she would catch the hint. I shook my head and ended the call. I just couldn't deal with her right now so I added her to my block list. Now none of her calls or text messages would come through. *I should have left her ass in Detroit.* I thought to myself.

I don't know what the fuck I was thinking moving her up here. If I was going to fuck off I should have just gotten all new bitches. Now this bitch act like she's falling in love or some shit. I pushed thoughts of her to the back of my mind so I could figure out what we were about to do about all this shit. We had to get rid of a body and find Tamia, all while being at war with the fucking unknown!

Tamia is definitely at the top of the list; I just don't know where to start looking.

"Man I hope nothing happens to her." I said out loud as I made my way out of the stairwell door.

I walked back inside of Armani's place without knocking. I needed to move fast and get rid of the body because it was starting to stink.

"Where the baby?" I asked because Candy and Armani were just sitting around.

"Asleep." Armani said and I nodded my head.

"Clean the fucking blood up then!" I snapped at her. She rolled her eyes but got up and followed me into the bathroom to get the cleaning supplies.

"Rashard-" she paused when I looked up at her. "About earlier. I'm-"

"Just don't let it happen again." I said cutting her off. If there was one thing I didn't have time for, it was discussing why she stood in the doorway playing in her pussy with her baby in arms while I cut the fingertips off her lover's wife.

Amere

     I drove around for a while as I tried to figure out if I wanted to go see Tamia or not. We had been texting back and forth for the last couple of hours and she had given me the address to where she was staying with Armani. The only reason that I hadn't gone yet was because I didn't want to run into Armani and have her fall off the good girl act. I said it was an act because the way she's been acting is not her. Tamia was convinced that she had changed though. She told me all about the fight they had and how that alone seemed to have solved all of their problems, but I guess we shall see. Tamia had quit texting me and I didn't know why, so I was tempted to pull up on her. My pockets being dry is what stopped me. I know she has gotten used to having a nigga with money, so I have to get my money up to fuck with her. I'm not saying she's gold digger and you know the rest. I have asked her plenty of times what Rashard does, but she never tells me. She doesn't even speak about them at all, so I have to read in between the lines. I know it wasn't a coincidence that when they moved to Atlanta, the streets of Detroit ran dry though. So I know what he does for money, I just can't believe Tamia is with him considering that fact.

I drove to the address my cousin Meech gave me and shut the engine off. When I climbed out of my car, the front door flew open and out came three niggas with their guns drawn. I shook my head and kept right on walking to the door. *"These niggas must be in training or something."* I thought to myself. Only a nigga that ain't been trapping long, comes out the door like that. I mean who the fuck they think they're scaring especially when I can see the short one's gun is on safety. That nigga ain't killing nobody.

"Aye Meech." I called out once I got within arm's reach of the guys in front of me. I waited for Meech to come out the door with a big Kool-Aid grin on his face.

"What's up cuzzo?" He asked with a welcoming smile. "Put y'all damn guns down." I said as I walked between them and dapped Meech up.

We walked inside and Meech filled me in on the war that was brewing in the streets. I couldn't help but think that I came at the wrong damn time. I'm not trying to be in no damn street war with mufuckers that I don't know. Shit from the sound of it, Meech don't even know. For all he knows, it could be his crew trying to take him out so they won't need him. He explained how Shard was helping him get his team together which explained the way they came out of the house.

"I guess he didn't show y'all how to take yall guns off safety." I said as I looked at the one named Peanut.

I wasn't trying to throw shade or anything like that but he's getting help from a behind the scenes ass nigga. Yea he was running shit with an iron fist back in Detroit but nobody knew who was running what.

He had a little smooth operation going and I don't know how he did it but he wasn't living this type of street life. I can't even say for sure if this nigga has ever been in a war, so how can he help them prepare for one? If anything, his ass got too much going on to be involving himself in this street shit. He don't know nobody here but Meech so he can't run shit from underground. Not to mention, if he gets Meech's crew together, which would have been something Meech couldn't do. The crew will respect him more. One thing you don't want is a crew that's more loyal to another mufucker. They will question everything you say and listen to him without a second thought. That's not the kind of organization you want to build. I pulled Meech to the side and told him just that too.

"You know him?" Meech asked as he looked at me suspiciously.

"Yeah. Rashard." I answered as I matched his stare. I was trying to see where this conversation was going.

"How you know him? You worked for him or something?" Meech asked and I shook my head.

"Why you asking?" I asked just as suspicious as he was looking at me.

"Man you sound a little salty. How you know him?" He asked and I shook my head.

The last thing I wanted him to think was that I was hating on Rashard. That wasn't the case. I was just letting him know some shit based on personal experiences but I see where this is going.

"He's with Tamia." I answered and regretted it before it ever left my lips. I know I sounded like a hating ass nigga that was just mad because he took my girl.

In all actuality, he didn't take her. I lost her. She met him long after the fact and they got together. I'm not salty because they're together. I know it won't last. What's meant to be will always be and they weren't meant to be.

"Naw I know Tamia. Yo high school girlfriend?" Meech asked just to be clear. I nodded my head but he kept shaking his. "Naw fam he's with Natasia. She moved up here not long after him. She bad too my nigga. All the niggas want her but she makes it clear who she's with." Meech explained.

I couldn't do anything but shake my head. This man got the best woman in the world at his disposal at home. A woman that doesn't need him, she simply wants him and nobody knows about her. That mean Tamia can be out doing her thing on the side and nobody will know to tell him. Meanwhile, he got this bitch on the side who probably needs him for everything that the streets know about. My girl can't catch a break but I promise, if I ever get her back she won't need nobody but me.

A few hours later, a whole bunch of niggas pulled up. I stood up and looked out the window but I didn't recognize any of them. They really didn't even look like some niggas from the A to be honest.

"Say cuzzo you know these cats?" I asked as I used my pistol to look out of the blinds.

Meech walked to the window slowly. Too slow for his ass to be a leader then relaxed visibly so I knew he was scared at first.

"They're part of Shard's crew." Meech said then opened the door. I shook my head because he didn't realize that after this shit, if Rashard wants to, he can take over the streets now that he has brought his crew in.

Meech has foolishly welcomed this man along with his crew into his city. If they start selling the product here that they had there, man it's going to be RIP to Meech's crew. It's like he's welcoming the takeover. One thing my mama used to tell me when I was in the streets real heavy, is to watch your friends first because they can do a whole lot more damage than your enemy can. See it's easy to beat your enemy because their intentions are clear. Now your friends…. your friends get close to ya, they learn ya weaknesses, then they exploit them.

The one I learned named was Deuce, phone started to ring. As he listened to the person on the other end, he had a deep scowl on his face. He looked like he was ready to kill everybody breathing after he hung his phone up.

"Let's roll out." He commanded and everybody stood up including Meech and his crew.

I shook my head as I followed suit. I had no idea what was going on but I wasn't taking my shit to get shot the fuck up in case it was that kind of party.

Michelle

I stared at the closed door in confusion until I heard low, deep growls behind me. I turned around slowly and came face to face with not one, not two but three Pitbull dogs. I wanted to scream but my voice got lodged in my throat. My neck, back and underarms started itch as I began to sweat profusely. They continued to growl as they made a slow creep towards me. I didn't know what to do besides run and I didn't know how fast I could run.

I made eye contact with the one in the middle and it had slob dripping out the corners of its mouth. I didn't know if it was hungry and ready to eat me or if it had rabies. Both were enough to make me haul ass. As soon as I took off, they took off. Surprisingly, I ran off pretty fast. There were four cars in the wrap around driveway. I just needed to make it to one of them. I didn't look back because I could hear the dogs barking loudly behind me. I came up to a four door sedan and jumped on the trunk. I ran to the top of the car and glanced back just as one of the pit bulls jumped on the car behind me. "Fuck!" I screamed out because I was tired. I ran down the opposite end of the car and jumped from it to the SUV that was parked right in front of it.

"Bitch you trying to get us killed!" Missy said out of nowhere.

Normally I would say something smart but we needed her to survive.

"What to do?" I yelled as I damn near slipped off the SUV as I climbed up the back of it.

"Kill them!" She screamed and I shook my head.

"These crazy ass pit bulls gone kill me first!" I snapped at her as I sat on top of the SUV. I watched the dogs jump all over each in an attempt to get to me.

Fear gripped my chest because I had no idea what to do. I felt like I was being watched so I looked around but I didn't see anyone. I glanced up at the windows and everybody was looking out of one. I shook my head as I realized to them, this was all a joke.

"Kill them. Kill them all!" Missy screamed. I shook my head because I didn't know how to go about killing all of them. Especially Silk's big ass. He could most definitely take me out without trying.

"I'm going to leave you just like your dad." Missy said. I saw red. Suddenly, I remembered the knives that I tied to my ankles using a shoelace. I snatched the knives off and laced my shoes up properly. It was now their time to go.

I laid flat on my stomach on top of the SUV, patiently, waiting on my chance to strike. The dogs continued to jump at me. I timed it perfectly as my knife went into one of dog's ear. It fell down howling out in pain. I smiled wickedly as I held up three fingers so they could see. The wounded dog scurried away as it whimpered in pain. I noticed it kept falling over so it must be off balanced. The remaining two dogs stopped jumping at me but the growling never ceased. I was no longer afraid. I now understand the phrase "It's either you or me". It won't be me.

I jumped off the truck and landed right between the vicious Pit bulls. I growled at them in an animalistic way. One of the dogs cocked its head to the side in confusion as it stared at me. Without further ado, I stabbed it in the neck over and over. Its blood spurted all over my face and clothes but I finally felt like myself again. I was no longer hurting from the beating Medusa put on me a few hours ago.

I looked up at the window and held up two fingers with a bright smile on my face. I walked around the yard as I followed the sound of soft whimpers until I found the dog that was already wounded. I grabbed his ear and pulled his head back as far it would go and slit his throat. I smiled as I watched the blood spurt out like water out of hose when there's a hole in it. An evil sadistic laugh came from the pit of my soul. I didn't recognize the sound as it bolted from my mouth. I looked up at the window and held up one finger. Silk stared at me with a weird expression on his face. I winked at him and walked off to find the last dog. Big bitches were going to eat me alive and for that, they must die.

I walked around aimlessly until I heard low growls. I knew the dog was warning me that I was getting too close. The only problem was, I wanted to get closer. I was going to kill this dog because it was either me or him and I wasn't ready. I peeked around the corner slowly and a slow smile began to spread across my face. The dog was now cowering off in the corner but it was far too late for that.

"I'm sorry for… 2004! And I'm not gonna mess up no more!" I sang the old song that practically came out of nowhere.

I continued to sing as I made my way to the dog. It jumped slightly when I stepped on a stick. I slowed my pace just as she leaped at me. The bitch really jumped higher than my head. She yelped out in pain as she landed on top of the knives that I held up just before she fell on me. Blood poured from her wounds and slid down my arms. It was so warm and made me feel all fuzzy inside. I finally felt free. This is what I do. I drug the dog around to the front yard so Silk could see. His mouth was wide open. All of the dogs were dead, now it's their turn. I shrugged my shoulders and made my way to the front door.

I sighed a frustrated sigh because I couldn't open the door. I took my shirt off, wrapped it around my fist then punched the window over and over until all of the glass was out of my way.

"Ready or not?" I sang as I climbed through the window. "Here I come." I continued as I made my way down the hall.

This time I made sure I opened each door and walk in as I came to it.

"You can't hide." I continued to sing the song as I searched the room that I knew belonged to Trina.

"I'm gonna find you! And kill you slowly!" I finished singing as I looked under the bed.

Trina started screaming and kicking. I grabbed her ankle and pulled her from under the bed.

I had no idea where the strength came from but I loved it. It was almost as if Missy and I were finally one! I could think like us both combined with the strength of us both. I guess I just needed to embrace her. I felt a joy like no other as I raised both knives above my head. I smiled as I looked down at her with tears in her eyes.

"Please." She begged but her pleas landed on deaf ears. I stabbed her in the stomach with one of the knives.

She screamed out so I stabbed her in the mouth with the other one. I stayed next to her until she died. Once I was sure that she was no longer with us, I snatched my knives out of her body and left out of the room. I closed the door behind me and made my way to the next door.

"Oh Stephanie! Oh Stephanie! How long will it take to kill you?" I sang using the tune from that Oh Christmas tree song. When I walked inside of her room, she was sitting on her bed halfway under the cover. I smiled as I made my way to her. She snatched the covers over her head.

"Aaaaaahhhh!" I screamed out. "Not the cover! Please not the cover! Hide under anything but the cover!" I mocked fear. I could hear her crying under the cover like it could stop me from killing her.

I shook my head and snatched the cover off of her.

"Why are you doing this?" She asked with a shaky voice. I gave her a slight shoulder shrug after I pretended to think about it.

"I don't know it's just the way I am." I said in my best Eminem voice.

I dove on the bed with my knives extended. She didn't move or anything. I sighed in disappointment as I killed her. It was no fun. Who just gives up like that? I was very disappointed in her. I expected her to have more fight than that.

I walked out of her room and into the next room, Megan. I couldn't help but wonder where Ashley, the white girl, was. Lucky for her, she didn't come back here or she'd have to die right along with them.

"Megan gotta die, die, die, die, die, die. Hopefully you don't cry, cry, cry, cry, cry, cry. Just give me a good try, try, try, try, try, try." I sang in my best Rihanna voice as I looked for Megan.

I can admit that I need to work on that one a bit more because it didn't sound too good. I looked under the bed and in the closet and didn't see her. I walked in her bathroom and she wasn't there either. "Ugh!" I said out of frustration after I closed her bathroom door back. I saw movement out the corner of my eye. By the time I looked, it was too late. Megan was in the air and diving in my direction. I dove out of the way and she hit the floor with a loud thud. When I turned to look at her, she had hit her head on the corner of the TV mount on her way down.

"Well damn." I said out loud because she had killed herself. I walked over to her and flipped her body over just to make sure she was dead. I couldn't really tell and I didn't have time to check for a pulse. I quickly stabbed her in the eye and snatched my knife back out.

"Fuck killing Tamia." I said out loud to myself. This shit was way more exhilarating.

Shit, fucking with Tamia always seemed to backfire any fucking way. I'd rather go around killing random people like I've been doing this past year. After all, I've never been more happier. Now if I could just get completely off the police's radar I'd definitely live it all the way up.

When I left out of the Megan's room, I followed the white carpet into a room filled with files. I walked around and threw the paperwork all over the room. I didn't care to read any of the shit but I didn't want to leave the shit all neat and clean either. I walked around to the desk and sat down. That's where I found a loaded .45, a cigar and lighter. I leaned back in the chair, placed the gun on the desk, propped my legs next to the gun and fired up the cigar. I started to choke and cough so much that my throat burned. My eyes started to water.

"Fuck!" I said in between coughs as I tried desperately to catch my breath. I threw the cigar in an attempt to get the smoke away from my face.

After a few minutes of coughing, it was like the smoke got worse. When I stood up straight, I saw the curtains were on fire. "Oops!" I said with a shrug of my shoulders. I walked out of the room and into the hallway.

"Silk! Medusa!" I called out but got no response. "Are you here?" I continued to yell.

"Just leave!" Medusa yelled back. I could hear faint bickering between her and Silk but I couldn't hear what they were saying.

"The roof. The roof. The roof is on fire! We don't need no water let that mufucker burn!" I chanted on my way back past the room.

The fire had completely engulfed that entire room. From the sound of their voices being near, I'd say they were about to be burned alive. I guess they'll figure it out eventually. I climbed back out of the window and made my way down the long drive way. I knew the gates wouldn't just open so I guess I'm going to have to climb over.

Rashard

I sat on the couch in the living room while I waited on my boys to get here. I knew the only person that would come up would be Deuce, so I needed to forewarn Candy. She was already sitting there looking crazy. I didn't want her anger to be directed towards me.

"Candy, Deuce fina come up here." I said straight up just to get it out there.

Candy and I have been friends forever so she knows me. I've never been good at beating around the bush. It's so much easier to just put it all on the table. She looked at me, rolled her eyes then shook her head.

"Did you ask him to fly out here?" She asked as she gave me a stank look. You would have thought I farted the way she was looking at a nigga.

"He followed you out here." I answered as I looked at her.

I know she's going to be happy when she sees those divorce papers. They both already signed them they just hadn't turned them in yet. Shit actually, he made her sign them before he boarded a plane to come here. He's not going to leave until Candy is ready to leave and be with him. Hell I bet if she wanted to move here, he would drop everything for her and move here without a second thought.

She shook her head at me and tears welled up in her eyes. I got up and sat next to her.

"That nigga love you Candy forreal." I said to her as I wrapped my arms around her. The tears started rolling down her cheeks at a rapid pace as she laid her head on my chest.

"What did you do for Tamia to leave you?" Candy asked and it caught me off guard.

"Tamia ain't left a nigga." I said with my face twisted up.

"Shit! Why you think we were all here? She was leaving you today. Lucky you she got kidnapped first." Candy said as if she was making light of the situation. Shit wasn't funny because I didn't have her back yet.

I thought about why she would want to leave me. It could be one of two things, I been cheating or because I threatened to put her out. When I told Candy that, she slapped me. Before I could respond, there was a knock at the door. Candy sucked her teeth as I walked past her. I opened the door and Deuce walked in with a large suitcase. I took it from him and went to the bathroom.

It took me about fifteen minutes to break her bones enough so she could fit inside of the luggage. I grabbed the handle and rolled it to Armani's room. She laid across her bed with Armad lying next to her as tears rolled down her face. I had no idea why she was crying but I honestly didn't care enough to try and figure it out.

"Get dressed. Roll this suitcase to the alley behind this building and set it on fire. Stay with it until it burns completely." I explained to her. I spoke clearly with precision so she would understand exactly what needed to be done.

"And what are you going to be doing?" She asked like I killed this bitch.

She really had some nerve questioning me when she's the reason this lady is dead in the first fucking place.

"Looking for Tamia." I stated as I stared at her.

I could see sadness wash over her face but it was replaced with anger. I gave her a confused look as I waited for her to respond. She climbed off the bed and started to rummage through her drawers for some clothes to put on.

"When you get her back safe." She said then paused once I made it to the door. "Don't cheat again." She said and I stopped in my tracks.

"Was she really about to leave me?" I turned around and asked.

I grabbed my chest as Armani nodded her head. There's no way she really loves me if she was going to leave me because she thinks I'm cheating. She don't have any proof so she can't just up and leave.

"I wasn't cheating." I lied with a straight face.

"Yeah that's why you're rarely home and when you come home, you accuse her of cheating but you show up smelling like you just hopped out the shower. Then threaten to put her out on her ass!" She said then turned and looked at me.
I felt like shit as I stared at her. I couldn't even say shit back to her.

"Nobody wants to live like that. Just an FYI, Tamia doesn't stick around when she doesn't want to. She can love you with every breath in her body but she won't stay if she's not happy." Armani said.

It felt like my whole spirit left as she broke Tamia down to me. To be perfectly honest, I don't think Tamia would ever leave me. Well let me rephrase that, I didn't think she would ever leave me.
Now the reason I felt like that is because she should have left after Chardae showed up at our old house. Well actually she did, but she shouldn't have

returned. Man I been fucking off with Natasia since right before we moved up here and so far Tamia has no clue. I'm positive when I find her that I can bring her back home because all she has are assumptions. I can tell her I took a shower at Meech's trap house and came home. I'm going to beg and plead to get her back but this time, I'm going to do right and that's on everything I love.

I turned around and left out of the room. Deuce and Candy were talking in the living room. Well Deuce was talking and Candy was listening. I'm not really sure if she was listening because she wasn't even looking at him.

"Bruh I'm going out the door. Gotta hit these streets and find out where Tamia is." I said and headed out the door. A few seconds later, he followed suit.

We hopped on the elevator and made our way down to the lobby. When I made it out to Deuce's car I couldn't believe my eyes.

"Why you got them?" I asked Deuce once I saw he brought Meech and his crew. There was a new body in the car but I couldn't see him.

"The more bodies the better." Deuce said with a shrug of his shoulders.

He had no idea that these niggas weren't worth the effort of bringing along. It was just too much trouble to try to keep them alive while staying alive. I nodded my head because he was about to find out just why I asked him that. I hopped in his car and we rode back to Meech's trap house. I had to do a double take when Amere stepped out of Meech's car.

I knew that it wasn't the time but shit, I wasn't about to be in this nigga's presence. Especially when he still been texting my girl. I know you wondering how I know but shit I check her shit every time she goes to sleep.

Tamia is an open book, so I know all of her passwords and she doesn't care. She doesn't lead him on or anything so I'm sure she doesn't think nothing is wrong with them conversing. Anytime you texting a nigga that wants you and is letting you know, you need not to text that nigga. What I couldn't figure out though was why he would ask about me all the fucking time. That's what was really pissing me off but Tamia never discussed our personal business or my personal business. She either wouldn't respond to the message or she would tell him some slick shit like the best part about business is minding your own.

I mugged the fuck out of him as everybody made their way to the door. I hung back so I could pull him to the side. As soon as Tre walked inside the house, I tapped Amere on the shoulder. He sighed once he noticed it was me. Tre nodded his head at me and closed the door.

"What's up?" Amere asked like everything was all good.

"Leave my girl alone." I stated as I looked at him. "Stop texting her phone. Move on playa. She's missing and the only reason you're still here is because you may be able to help us find her." I said then waited for him to respond.

He smiled at me but not a small smile. This nigga smiled real big as he looked at me then shook his head. I mugged the fuck out of buddy and he started laughing. My blood started to boil and my trigger finger started itching.

"What's funny?" I asked him.

"I'm just confused that's all." He said then shrugged his shoulders. "I don't know Natasia so how am I texting her?" He asked with a serious expression on his face.

I began to wonder how he knew about her and if he had told Tamia. This nigga just signed his death certificate and didn't even know it.

"Touché." I said as I turned around and walked inside of the house. All eyes were on me as everyone awaited my orders.

Armani

1 week later

It's been a whole week and there has been no sign of Tamia. Rashard and his crew been combing the streets day in and day out in an attempt to find her but with no luck. I've been worried sick and I was wishing I hadn't allowed her to go out of the door alone. All I was thinking about was Armad though and I knew Tamia's heart was in the right place when she decided to go talk to him alone. She knew that if he had tried to kill Candy and Rashard's little sister once, that he wouldn't hesitate to do it again. What I couldn't figure out though was how did he find out where she was. It sure beat the hell out of me, because I couldn't for the life of me figure out if there was a snake among us. How all of a sudden the night Candy shows up, Brandon show up as well? I sat on the couch across from Candy as I fed Armad and stared at her. I desperately wanted answers and I was going to get them.

"Why'd you do it?" I asked because I've never been one to beat around the bush. She looked at me with a confused expression on her face but I wasn't buying the act.

"Why'd you lead Brandon here?" I asked her and her mouth fell open. "Yea you didn't think nobody would figure it out huh? What he promised he wouldn't hurt you if you showed him where she was?" I asked with a frown on my face.

Shit I thought Candy was a good person before I figured out that she was the one who lead Brandon here.

"I didn't even know he was alive and I would never lead him to Tamia!" She snapped at me. I sucked my teeth then rolled my eyes at her.

"Do you know what I went through the day he damn near killed me?" She asked in an attempt to get sympathy.

"Who gives a fuck Candy?! The only reason you lead him here is so you wouldn't have to go through whatever it was again." I said. I needed her to know that I was on to her. There was no putting shit past me. My phone went off and alerted me that I had a text message.

Tamia: Tell Rashard find Simone

"What the fuck?" I asked out loud as I pressed call to dial Tamia's number.

It rang once and her voicemail picked up. I hung up and called right back but it went right back to voice mail.

"What's wrong?" Candy asked with a worried expression on her face. Her ass should be an actress the way she's putting on a show.

"Wouldn't you like to know?!" I said with a roll of my eyes. I wanted to call Rashard but I didn't know his number. I couldn't tell Candy because I think she's working with Brandon.

I grabbed my son and walked out of the room and called Amere. It rang three times then went to voicemail. I sighed heavily and tried again and it still went to voicemail. I was beyond frustrated. "Ugh!" I screamed out as fresh tears stung my cheeks. Before I knew what was happening, Candy snatched Armad out of my hand and walked away with him in hers. I followed her because if the bitch hurt my son then she was going to end up like Dave's wife.

Speaking of Dave, his ass has been calling me every day multiple times a day. I never answer the phone though because I don't want him to ask me any questions about his wife. I'm afraid I won't be able to lie to him if I talk to him.

I stood in the doorway and watched Candy lay Armad in his crib in a loving way. When she looked up at me, there wasn't a loving bone in her body. She charged at me and pushed me into the wall so hard that I lost my breath. I frowned and swung with all of my might. It was as if she was expecting that because she ducked just in a nick of time and punched me in the stomach on her way back up. I doubled over in pain and gripped my stomach. She grabbed my hair and pulled me towards the living room. I lost my balance and fell but she didn't stop pulling until we were in the middle of the living room floor.

I swung my arms at her wildly and not one blow landed on her. She kicked me in the side and I cried out in pain. I used my arms to wrap around my body in a failed attempt at soothing the pain. She reached down and folded my arms across my stomach then sat on top of them.

"I don't want to fight you." She said as she breathed heavily in my face. I was beyond confused because if she didn't want to fight then why did she attack me. "But I will and I will win." She said and gave me the side eye. "I will hurt you Armani. If you didn't have that baby, I would kill you." She said then slapped me so hard that my head rocked to the other side.

Both sides of my face hurt because the impact from her blow sent my face into her shoe. I could feel my eye throbbing and I knew it would be swollen in no time.

"See I think you forgot that you're the jealous friend that secretly wants her life not me! I love Tamia as if she was my sister and I wouldn't dare do anything to cause harm to anyone I love." She said.

I noticed her facial features softened as she continued to explain.

"That day Brandon came to my house looking for Tamia, I refused to tell him where she was or when she was coming back. He thought he could beat it out of me Armani. As I laid on the floor seeing black spots, I still didn't tell him she was at her graduation and would be back shortly! I could barely breathe as I watched his foot slam down into me over and over but I still didn't open my mouth!" She said then paused.

By this time, she was crying and trying to regroup so she could continue. I was at a loss for words. Never had I ever met a person like Candy. Truth be told, he would have only had to slap me once and I would have told him exactly where she was. Hell who am I kidding, back then all he would have had to do was ask and he would have known everything he needed to know. I would have been like "Man she has on a multi colored maxi dress underneath her royal blue graduation gown. She sitting in between such and such and such and such on the third row from the back!" In other words, it would have taken little to nothing for me to give Tamia up because I am the jealous friend that secretly wanted her life. I've changed though. Her life ain't no better than anyone else's. She goes through it just like the rest of us.

"As I stared down the barrel of his gun, I still didn't tell him anything! Now I'm only going to ask you this once Armani. What did that message say?" She said as she looked down at me.

I could tell by the look on her face that she meant business. If I couldn't even get a lick in when she didn't want to fight me, I didn't want to try when she actually wanted to.

"Tell Rashard to find Simone." I answered as I stared up at her. I could tell she was confused but she got up and grabbed her phone.

Tamia

I regretted my decision as soon as Brandon through me in the trunk of his car. We rode around for hours and I had no idea where he was taking me. When we finally made it to our destination it was dark again. I couldn't believe I rode in the trunk of a car all of that time. When Brandon came around and popped the trunk, we were in a garage. I rolled my eyes because I had no way of knowing where he had taken me too.

We walked in the house but I was blindfolded until I was led into a room. It was a fairly nice room. Who am I kidding? The room was big as fuck and had a bathroom in it. I heard Brandon and some chick argue quite a bit. She didn't want me here but at the same time she hadn't done anything to help me get out.

I had managed to get out of the room a few times and look around the house. It was a really nice house but it had taken me a week of sneaking out to catch them slipping. She had finally left her mail sitting on the counter. I had only had a chance to glance at it before Brandon snatched me up and threw me back in the room, literally. I was able to figure out that her name is Simone and that I was still somewhere in Atlanta.

I don't quite understand why Brandon wanted me here with him when he only came in here with me when it was time for us to eat. We had been eating breakfast, lunch and dinner together in my room since I been here. He only hurt me once and that was today when he tossed me back into my room. I still had my cell phone because the dummy never searched me. I just had it powered off.

I knew I needed to call Rashard, but pride wouldn't let me ask for help. Not to mention, it was one of those cheap phones since I broke my IPhone and he wouldn't be able to find me. I powered my phone on and texted Armani to tell her what to tell Rashard. The only reason I texted her and not Candy is because her name was first in my contact list and I didn't know when Brandon would be bursting back into my room. Now I just needed to play it cool until Rashard found me.

As I sat on the bed with a smile on my face reality set in. Not one time had I ever needed Rashard and he came through. Each time it was always Brandon who had been my superman. Now I couldn't help but think who could save me from him.

"Amere." I said out loud to myself. I powered my phone back on and dialed his number. I walked in the bathroom as the phone rang and rang then the voicemail picked up.

"Fuck!" I cursed as I leaned my body against the bathroom door. I locked the door and sat against it. "C'mon Amere please answer." I said out loud as the phone rang.

"Tamia?" He called out.

BANG! BANG! BANG! "OPEN THE FUCKING DOOR NOW!!" Brandon screamed from the other side of the door.

The impact of his blows caused the door to hit me and I accidentally dropped my phone. I crawled over to it as fast as I could. When I picked it up the screen was completely black. I tried to power it back on but it wouldn't work. "Nooo." I said completely defeated. I shook my head as hot tears began to sting my cheeks. I slid the phone away from me and crawled over inside of the tub. Brandon kicked the door so hard that it flew off of its hinges. I ducked down with my eyes closed to keep debris from hitting me as wood fragments landed all over me in the tub. I felt my body being snatched out of the tub roughly.

"Stop!" I screamed as I swung and clawed at his face.

My blows were rendered useless against his muscular frame. He hit my head on the door panel on our way out of the bathroom then threw me on the floor.

"Who did you call?!" He asked as he stared down at me with rage filled eyes. I scooted away from him slowly as he approached me. I shook my head as I wiped the tears from my face.

He walked over to me swiftly and kicked me so hard that my body rose off the ground then landed with a thud. I cried out in pain. I begged him to stop but it was of no use. I held my hand up and he stomped it down with his foot. I knew my finger was broken by the way it laid crooked as I allowed my hand to rest on my chest. He got down on his knees and punched me over and over in the face. I sent up a silent prayer that the lord would take me now. I began to see black dots through my blurred vision then everything faded to black.

Rashard

"What's up sis?" I answered the phone. Candy hadn't called at all since we been looking for Tamia. We been turning shit upside down trying find her to but it was like she had disappeared without a trace. I was starting to think that he had possibly taken her out of Atlanta.

"Find Simone." She said.

I pulled the phone away from my ear to make sure it was Candy talking.

"Who is that?" I asked clearly confused.

"She has Tamia." Candy said then disconnected the call. Candy has never been one to talk on the phone and when she does, she never says much.

I stuck the phone back in my pocket and walked into the living room where everybody else was. For some reason, Meech had been acting a bit salty these last couple of days. I think it's because his crew has been taking orders from Deuce. Don't get me wrong, Atlanta is ripe for the picking but I don't want it. Deuce doesn't even live here so I don't think he wants it. Plus, I'm sure he would have said something to me first. If Meech was an actual leader, his crew would hesitate to take orders from another one but they been dick riding since they got here.

Now if Deuce decided to move here, it would be nothing for him to come in and take shit right from underneath Meech's nose. For one, Meech's product ain't worth a bitch ass thing. For two, we already have a few established connects. All we would have to do is fly our runners out here every other week to keep the streets of Atlanta juicing. Once our product floods the streets, the smokers will flock to us like flies to shit.

"What happened?" Deuce asked once he saw the look on my face.

"Candy said a bitch name Simone has Tamia." I said to him.

"How she know that?" Deuce asked. I shrugged my shoulders. He knows as well as I know that Candy ain't give that much information out over the phone.

"Who you say got her?" Meech asked with his eyebrow raised.

"Tamia?" Amere yelled into his phone. I didn't answer Meech's question because I was waiting on Amere to finish his phone call.

All eyes zoomed in on him as he yelled her name over and over.

"Fuck!" He said as he dialed her number again and again.

"What happened?" I asked as I walked right up to him.

"We got disconnected." He said as he shook his head. My mind went straight to trying to figure out why she called him and not me.

I know I read those messages and she wasn't giving him no play. Maybe she deleted the messages she sent him that would piss me off.

My blood started to boil and I started to breathe heavy. I felt a hand on my shoulder but I snatched away.

"Bro not now." Deuce said. He knew I was ready to kill this nigga. Deuce and I had already had this conversation.

"Who is Simone?" I asked Amere.

He looked confused at first then he looked over at Meech. All my anger instantly went towards Meech. Why would he know who Simone is?

"Nigga you been holding her?" Amere asked Meech then charged at him. He didn't give him time to respond as he slammed him on the floor.

"We been murking mufuckers and you got her?" Amere asked then slammed his fist into Meech's face. I looked around the room and none of Meech's crew tried to intervene.

I grabbed Amere in a bear hug and pulled him away from Meech so he could tell us what he knew. Amere tried and tried to break free from my grasp but he couldn't. I looked back at Tre and signaled for him to get Meech up. He walked around and snatched Meech up off the floor.

"Where my girl at?" I asked Meech.

"Man I don't know what y'all talking about." He said as he mugged Amere while rubbing his jaw.

"He lying! Simone his sister!" Amere screamed. I let him go and pulled out my pistol. I was not about to play with this nigga at all especially not when it came to Tamia.

"Where my girl at Meech?" I asked then cocked my pistol.

"I swear iono man." He said then spit out blood.

"I know." Amere said as he mugged Meech right back.

I sent two bullets to Meech's dome and watched his body drop to the floor.

"Man what the fuck man? You could have warned me!" Tre said clearly pissed because he got blood on his clothes.

I gave him a shoulder shrug and turned to Amere. He was stuck on stupid with his mouth wide open.

"Why you kill him?" He asked as he stared down at his lifeless body.

"Never pull a gun out on a nigga unless you about to use it." I stated plainly then headed out the door. Everybody followed suit. Amere came out last shaking his head.

"Lead the way." I told him.

I can't believe this man killed my cousin. He killed him right in front of me and his crew and nobody did a thing. I warned him about that nigga and he didn't listen. I let anger cloud my judgement when I accused him and now he's dead. Then this nigga gone give me that bullshit ass excuse about why he killed him. Man I know Meech would have understood why he pulled a gun out on him and there would have been no hard feelings. This man killed my cousin and for that, I have to kill him. When this is all over with, he will be on the other side of my gun. He will die. He just doesn't know it yet.

I walked out of the house and hopped in my car. I hope like hell I remembered how to get there because I hadn't been there since I left. The crazy thing is, if Tamia is there, Simone hasn't been acting like it. I've been calling and checking in with her so she wouldn't be worried and she was always in good spirits. When I turned on her street, I parked my car in the driveway. Everybody else parked on the side of the street. I climbed out of the car and walked up to the door. I knocked and waited patiently for her to answer. Again, she opened the door with an attitude while wearing workout attire.

"Did I interrupt your workout again?" I asked and her hand flew to her mouth.

As I stood there looking at her, I had completely forgotten about our reason for being here.

"What are you doing here?" She stammered as she began to step from one foot to the other like she had to pee. I frowned slightly as I stared at her.

"I'm living here." I reminded her as she positioned her body between the door and the frame.

"Now is not a good time." She said. I could see beads of sweat rolling down her forehead as she stared at me.

"You got company?" I asked.

"No!" She said in a high pitched voice.

Before I could respond, Rashard pushed his way from behind me, into the house.

"Who are you?" She asked Rashard. He didn't respond as he punched her in the mouth.

Ooohs and Aaahs could be heard from behind us. This nigga never ceases to amaze me. I couldn't believe he had just knocked her ass out.

Her body lay limp on the floor in the spot she once stood. I leaned over, scooped her up and carried her to her living room couch. I was still in shock at what he had just done.

"POW! POW! POW!"

The sound of gunshots snapped me out of my state of shock as I watched Rashard grab his shoulder and run back out of the room.

"LEAVE NOW OR I'LL KILL HER!!" I heard someone yell from the back.

Peanut and Skeme ran in the house with their guns drawn. I grabbed them to make sure the shit wasn't on safety. They were good so I let them go.

"Let her go or I'mma kill this bitch in here!" Rashard screamed back.

I knew if it was up to him to save Tamia, she'd end up hurt because he's just too fucking reckless. I made my way to the back of the house with Tre and Deuce hot on my heels.

"You outnumbered cuzzo just let her go." Deuce screamed.

I was beyond confused. I didn't know Tamia got kidnapped by Deuce's cousin. If that's the case, then why is he still breathing and my cousin is dead? I shook my head at the bullshit because I'm going to kill them both.

"Deuce? That you?" The guy yelled.

"Yeah B, it's me. This ain't gotta end bad. As long as you don't hurt her you will live." Deuce said and I couldn't help but think that his loyalty should be with his family yet he's siding with Rashard.

Everybody waited for Brandon to respond. Silence. Rashard signaled for Skeme to come to him. As soon as Skeme past the door, Brandon started shooting. I don't know how many times Skeme was hit but he dropped like a bad habit. I shook my head at the shit mufuckers go through because of their love for a bitch. There's not a soul on the planet that I'd die for. When Peanut saw Skeme on the floor, he took off in his direction.

POW! CLICK! CLICK! CLICK!

Brandon's gun was empty. Rashard took that chance to run back to the door but Brandon kicked the door closed.

POW! POW!

Rashard shot the doorknob off the door and kicked it in.

"Where are you pussy?" Rashard called out as he walked in the room.

"Put the gun down and fight like a man!" Brandon yelled out. "The best man gets to keep her." He continued to scream from where ever he was hiding in the room.

"Alright." Rashard said and I heard his gun hit the floor.

Shock was an understatement as I stood in the doorway and watched Brandon walk out of the bathroom with a smile on his face. I glanced over at the bed and noticed Tamia was laying there completely still with a battered and bruised face. I shook my head. I stared at her until I noticed she was starting to stir. The glimmer of something shiny caught my eye. I turned and saw Brandon had something in has hand as he approached Rashard. I didn't warn him because I wanted Brandon to kill him.

POW!

Rashard pulled a gun from out of fucking nowhere and shot Brandon in his chest. I watched him fall to his knees as blood poured out of his mouth.

I got pissed off instantly because I didn't expect the shit to be that quick and easy. I sighed dramatically as I watched Rashard walk over to Tamia like he had just saved the day.

Tamia

As I opened my eyes I couldn't believe the first person I saw was Rashard. For the first time, he had saved my life. I smiled up at him as he rubbed my face.

"I know you been talking to that nigga but I still love you." He said and I scrunched my face up. Out of all the things he could have said to me, he chose to say that.

I looked past him and saw Amere standing there so I guess Amere told him we had been texting. In all honesty it was just on a friend type level as I said before. Oh well, I'm glad he told him because maybe now he'll be the man I need him to be instead of the man in the streets.

"Where's Brandon?" I asked as I tried to sit up. My head started to hurt something serious so I leaned my body against Rashard. He wrapped his arms around me and helped me stand to my feet.

I saw Brandon laying on the floor gurgling on his own blood. It was like déjà vu, only I had shot him in the back last time. I have no idea how he made it through that but he wasn't about to make it through this. I grabbed Rashard's gun out of his hand and walked over to Brandon. I used my foot to flip his body over. He stared straight up at me as he choked on his blood. I stared down at him as I willed myself to kill him because I knew if I didn't, he would keep coming back.

"I love you." He croaked out and that was the only push I needed.

POW!

One shot to his head silenced him forever. I couldn't believe this man told me he loved me.

"Fucking lunatic." I said out loud as Rashard wrapped his arms around me.

I nodded my head at Amere as we walked past him and headed out to the front door. When I saw Simone laid out on the couch, I stopped in my tracks.

"Is she dead?" I asked Rashard and he shook his head no. I limped over to her and used the couch for balance. I leveled the gun at her head and pulled the trigger.

"Why you do that?" Rashard asked once we were in the car.

"She helped him hide me." I stated as I leaned back and closed my eyes.

6 months later....

Rashard and I had been in complete bliss. He used some of his drug money to help me start my own practice, so I now owned my own clinic. I worked for myself, had employees and everything was going well.

Deuce and Candy ended up moving here and now he's basically running the streets. He even gave Amere a job and that shocked me completely.

Armani started dating the guy across the hall against my better judgement but she seems to be happy with it. His name is James Steele and I know that because him and Candy had had a brief exchange. He gives me a bad vibe so I tend to stay away from him. Armani has tried to tell me about the sex games he likes to play but it was just too weird.
Who the fuck has cards that tell you how long you should do certain sexual favors to the other one? I didn't even want to hear about no crazy shit like that, now she doesn't try to tell me. I just figured if she likes it then I love it. She can keep all the details to herself.

Any who, Rashard asked me to marry him. For some reason, I felt the need to talk to Amere about it first but he seemed ok with it. I don't even know why I told him.
Rashard has been coming home every night and he's getting ready to open up a club here in Atlanta. He has this brilliant plan that he thinks will steal all of the strippers from Diamonds of Atlanta.
That man really kills me. Our relationship has been so good since we've both been giving it our all. I swear you can't tell me nothing about my man. His ass doesn't even have a lock code on his phone anymore.

Well, I gotta go! Ya girl has a wedding to plan!

True Glory Publications

IF YOU WOULD LIKE TO BE A PART OF OUR
TEAM, PLEASE SEND YOUR SUBMISSIONS BY
EMAILTO
TRUEGLORYPUBLICATIONS@GMAIL.COM.
PLEASE INCLUDE A BRIEF BIO, A SYNOPSIS OF
THE BOOK, AND THE FIRST THREE CHAPTERS.
SUBMIT USING MICROSOFT WORD WITH FONT IN
11 TIMES NEW ROMAN.

Check out these other great books from True Glory Publications

Sins of Thy Mother

The Lyin` King

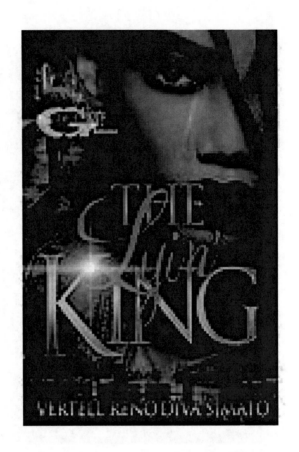

By Any Means Necessary

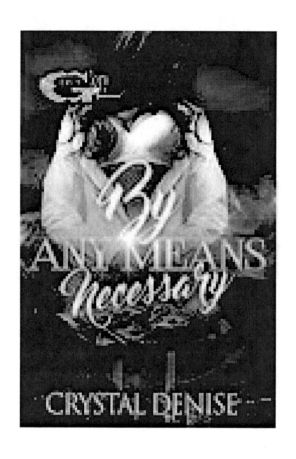

Mancell's Reign: Daughter of A Kingpin